MARRY ME

SAMANTHA LIND

SAMANTHALIND.COM

Marry Me
Lyrics & Love Series Book 1
Copyright © 2018 Samantha Lind
All rights reserved.

Cover Design by *Oh So Novel*

Editing by *All About The Edits*

Proofreading by *Proof Before You Publish*

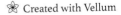 Created with Vellum

Renee

Thank you for your encouragement to write this book! I loved every time you messaged me telling me the song was following you as much as it was following me! Your encouragement throughout the entire process meant everything to me. I know you love Lauren & Sam just as much as I do, and I hope that never changes!

Thomas Rhett

I know the likelihood of you ever seeing these words is very slim, but on that off-chance that you do one day read this page, thank you. Thank you for writing such passionate words into songs. Thank you for loving your wife as deeply as you do that you have that passion to write such emotional songs.

When the idea for this book came to me, I'd heard "Marry Me" many times. But it was that one time, something changed. The words spoke to me in a way they never had before.

So, here's to you, and the love story you created with this song. I can only hope my inspiration has done it a fraction of the justice it deserves.

CONTENTS

A NOTE FROM THE AUTHOR

Sometimes an idea for a new book will strike an author out of thin air. They see a picture, live through an experience, hear a song, watch a commercial, you get the gist. That is exactly how this series and book came to existence.

I'd heard the song "Marry Me" by Thomas Rhett countless times, even watched the music video a few times (my kids are obsessed with watching music videos!) and nothing...until one evening, I was driving home with my kids when this song came on the radio and within minutes, I had the entire book plotted in my mind.

As soon as I got home that evening, I started jotting down the ideas and within an hour, I had everything set; I just didn't know when I'd be able to fit this book into my already-booked schedule. To my disarray, the characters for this book decided they were most important and pushed their way into the front of my mind, and wouldn't stop yelling at me until I sat down and wrote them out. Unfortunately for me, I was under a deadline for my last release at the time. So, like the good little author I am, I sat down and wrote out the first few chapters, and then put them on the back burner until I finished my other book.

From the moment I had the book plot pop into my mind, it's almost as if the song has been following me. For the week following that evening, every time I got into my car, the song would either already be on the radio or would be the next song played! It was almost a little freaky! But I embraced it and soon the ideas started flowing and I turned it not only into a new book but decided that since music influences all of us so much already, I would create an entire series of standalone books, where a song plays a role in bringing its character to life. These books will not overlap, they will just be under the *Lyrics and Love* umbrella, since they will be inspired completely by a song.

In closing, I leave you with the only song that inspired this book. The one I've now listened to on repeat probably over a thousand times while writing this book. The character and words really flowed once I was able to dedicate time to them and I hope you love it as much as I enjoyed writing it.

PLAYLIST

Marry Me ~ Thomas Rhett

1

SAM

Now

"WHISKEY, ON THE ROCKS. MAKE IT A DOUBLE," I TELL THE bartender as I collapse on the barstool.

"Yes, sir," the pretty blonde behind the bar replies, giving me a once-over.

As I wait for her to pour my drink, I tug on my tie, pulling it from my neck and stuffing it in my pocket, as my mind wanders to tomorrow.

The day I've dreaded since that envelope arrived at my apartment a few months ago.

Lauren.

She's getting married.

Tomorrow.

But instead of marrying *me,* she's marrying some *douchebag.* No, *I'm not bitter at all.*

"Sam!" I hear Steven call my name as he sits on the barstool next to me and slaps my shoulder.

The bartender slides my drink in front of me and sets

down a coaster in front of Steven. "What can I get for you?" she asks him as I pick up my whiskey and take a hefty drink.

"I'll take a Blue Moon, on tap if you have it."

"Sixteen or twenty-four ounce?" she asks.

"Might as well make it a twenty-four ouncer. Looks like I'll be here awhile," he tells her, motioning to me with a nod of his head.

My eyes follow the bartender as she walks off to fill Steven's order.

"So, you want to talk about it?" he questions, knowing full well that I've been in love with his sister for years.

She just doesn't know that.

"Not really, but I have a feeling you're not going to stop bugging me until we do," I reply, bringing my glass back to my lips. The whiskey burns as it slides down my throat and fills my belly. The only way I'm going to be able to make it through tomorrow is to be intoxicated. I just need to stay on this side of being obnoxiously drunk because the last thing I would want to do is ruin Lauren's wedding day.

Even if she is *marrying the douchebag.*

2

SAM

9 YEARS OLD

I WATCH WITH EXCITEMENT AS TWO MOVING TRUCKS PULL down our street and stop at the empty house across from ours. The old couple who had lived in that house for all of my nine years had sold it at the end of spring, and the new family was finally moving in.

Please have kids! I think to myself.

I watch with anticipation, hoping that a boy my age would climb out of one of the vehicles that followed the trucks in. But before anyone could get out of the van, one of the moving trucks blocks my view of the driveway.

"Sam, get your shoes on. It's time to leave," my mom yells.

"Yes, ma'am," I call out to her as I leave the window and go to get ready.

As we back out of the driveway, I keep my eyes glued to the neighbors' house, continuing my search for a playmate. Not many kids live on our street and being an only child, I get lonely often.

"When we get home from the store, you can come with me to welcome our new neighbors to the neighborhood, unless you'd like for me to drop you off at Grandma and Grandpa's, and you can come home later with Dad," my mom says, pulling my attention away as we drive out of our neighborhood.

"I'd rather come back home with you. I'm hoping that some kids moved in across the street."

My mom's errands take what feels like forever to finish, when it was probably only an hour or two tops.

As soon as we pull into the driveway, I see kids in the other yard.

Kids!

They are running through a sprinkler.

One boy. *Yes!*

One girl. *I can work with that.*

And best of all, they look about my age. *Even better!*

"Mom, Mom, can I go play with them? Please?" I practically beg.

"Help me bring in the groceries and then we can go introduce ourselves. If their parents are okay with it, then yes, you can play."

Jackpot!

I help my mom with the groceries with lightning speed; the excitement of meeting the new kids across the street fuels my eagerness to help get everything put away as fast as I can.

As soon as the last item is away, I bounce my way to the front door, ready to go.

"Wait just a second, Sam." My mom laughs. "Let me grab a plate of cookies to take with us."

As my mom assembles cookies on a plate and then covers it, I watch out the window as the kids play across the street.

"Okay, I'm ready if you are," Mom tells me as she stops in front of the door.

I open it for her and we head across the street.

As we approach the front door, my mom reaches out and rings the doorbell at the same time we hear the boy call out at us.

"Hey!"

"Hi!" I tell him. "I live across the street, and I was hoping to play with you guys."

The front door opens, and a tired-looking woman steps forward.

"Hello, I'm Amy and this is my son, Sam. We live just across the street and wanted to welcome your family to the neighborhood," my mom tells her, handing her the plate of cookies.

"Thank you so much. I'm Debra, and that's Steven and Lauren. My husband, Dave, is around here somewhere. How are you today, Sam?" she asks me.

"I'm great, thank you. Can I play with them?" I ask, nodding in the direction of the kids playing in the yard.

"Of course, go have fun."

I run off immediately, skidding to a halt in front of the boy and girl playing together, catching their attention.

"Hi, I'm Sam. Can I play with you guys?"

"Hi, I'm Steven, and this is my sister, Lauren. Do you want to run through the sprinkler with us?" Steven asks.

"I'll need to ask my mom and run home to change first," I tell him. She gives me the go-ahead, and I run home as fast as I can to change and get back outside to play with my new friends.

LAUREN, STEVEN, AND I PLAY IN THE SPRINKLER FOR WHAT feels like hours. We ran all over the yard, both theirs and my own, until we were worn out and starving. After a quick supper for all of us, we were back outside, playing until everyone had to get to bed.

"Today was the best day ever," I tell my parents as we talk before I climb into bed. "I can't believe I finally have friends that live so close!"

"It sure does appear we hit the jackpot with our new neighbors," my mom says. "I'm glad you had so much fun today with them, Sam."

"Can I play again with them tomorrow?"

"I'm sure you can. Just make sure to stay out of the way as Mr. and Mrs. Kramer are unpacking and trying to get everything put away inside the house."

"Yes, ma'am," I answer my mother. "Good night, I love you."

"Love you, too, Sam. Now off to bed. We have church in the morning."

I give her a hug before pulling the comforter over me and falling asleep with a smile on my face.

3

LAUREN

NOW

I SIT ALONE IN THE TENT THAT'S SET UP ON MY GRANDPARENTS' property. We used it tonight for the rehearsal dinner, and it will be used tomorrow night for my wedding reception. I look around at all the perfectly placed decorations. The magnolia flowers I've always dreamed about having at my wedding. The images I always dreamed of growing up, for what my perfect wedding would look like.

I've always wanted to get married in just this spot, having loved my grandparents' land since I was little. They once had thousands of acres but began to sell it off in large chunks over the years, keeping the area around the house for themselves, after neither my dad nor any of my aunts and uncle showed any desire in taking over the farm.

I stand and walk to the edge of the tent and look around, taking in the star-filled sky. The slight breeze feels good against my heated skin. Everything is perfect, except for this nagging feeling deep within me that has me wondering what is wrong. I keep pushing the feeling back, figuring it's just the normal wedding jitters and nothing more than that. I pull a chair to the edge and sit back down.

Tomorrow, I'm marrying the man I love.

The man I plan to start a family and grow old with.

As I think of these things, and what my life will look like five, ten, twenty-five years down the line, I don't see Brad.

I see Sam.

The man I've always loved, but he just doesn't love me the same way. He doesn't want to marry me.

I shake my head, hoping to clear the images of walking down the aisle to Sam.

Dancing with Sam.

Running away to a romantic honeymoon with Sam.

I don't even realize the tears have started to roll down my cheeks until one hits my hand that's sitting in my lap. I quickly swipe at the tears, not that anyone is out here with me. But if anyone was to come out, I don't want them to see me sitting here crying.

I take a few deep breaths, doing my best to calm myself down.

I sit in the moonlight awhile longer, thinking back to my childhood and all the good memories.

Lauren

9 years old

THE SUMMER HAD PASSED BY IN A BLUR. MY FAMILY MOVED into our new house at the beginning of the summer, and as much as I hated the idea at the time, it has been amazing.

Steven and I made fast friends with Sam. He fit in with the two of us, and we've been thick as thieves all summer.

School starts tomorrow, and the jitters of starting at a new school have been increasing all day. The excitement of meeting new friends and teachers is almost overwhelming. Sam has been assuring me that the school we'll be going to is great and I'll fit in easily, but I'm still nervous about it.

"Do you have your backpack all ready for tomorrow?" my mom asks, walking into my bedroom with a basket of clean clothes.

"Yes, I've packed and repacked it a few times, just to make sure I didn't forget anything."

Chuckling, she tells me, "You'll do great tomorrow, and it's not like you don't already have two built-in friends."

"I know," I say on a sigh. "I'm still nervous, but at least the three of us got put into the same class."

"I can't believe my babies are going to be in the fourth grade," Mom says, wrapping me in a hug.

"Well believe it, 'cause we're not getting any younger," I tease her.

"How about we head out for a girls' lunch, and maybe go get our nails done afterwards?" she suggests.

"Sure! I'll just put these clothes away quick, and then can be ready to go," I reply, hopping off my bed.

———

"HOW'D YOU LIKE YOUR FIRST DAY?" SAM ASKS ME AS WE ALL walk home from school.

"It was great! Mrs. Smyth was so nice, I'm really going to enjoy being in her class. I was just a little bummed you and Steven got switched into the other class. How was your first day?"

"It was good, and I told you that you'd love Mrs. Smyth. Did she give you any homework?"

"Nope, said we won't start homework until next week. She's easing us into it," I tell him, as a small laugh escapes my lips. "What about Mr. Lund, did he give you guys homework?"

"Just our reading logs for the month, so not really homework."

"Oh yeah, we got those, too."

"I'm going to go grab a snack, but after, do you guys want to play?" Sam asks Steven and me as we approach our houses.

"Yep, meet ya back outside in a few minutes," Steven tells Sam as he runs up and into our house.

"See ya in just a bit. I'm glad your first day was good," Sam says to me before he splits off and walks over to his driveway.

4

SAM

NOW

I LIE HERE IN MY HOTEL ROOM, STARING AT THE WHITE CEILING, thoughts of how I'm going to get through today going through my mind. Lauren is one of the most important people in my life, yet one of the hardest to be around. It's the main reason I took a job in North Carolina. I couldn't handle being around her all the time if she wasn't mine to hold.

Touch.

To call mine.

My mind wanders again, as it has been doing lately. This time, I recall that one day, back in high school...

Sam

16 years old

I SIT DOWN ON THE BENCH AND SLIDE MY HELMET OFF AS ONE of the student managers holds out a towel and water bottle to me. I grab both, and simultaneously take a refreshing drink as I sop the sweat from my face and neck. I'd just caught an incredible pass from Steven, running the ball in for a thirty-eight-yard touchdown and giving our team a seventeen-point lead with only four minutes left in the game.

I hear my name being called from behind me, by a voice I'd be able to pick out from any crowd.

Lauren.

I turn to find my best friend standing along the railing, a huge smile on her face as she waves at me. She turns, pointing to the back of her t-shirt that she's decorated with my name and number. I laugh and wave back at her before returning my attention to the game in front of me.

We hold off the other team from scoring, closing out our season undefeated. We're headed to the playoffs, but first, tonight, we're all going out to celebrate.

After hitting the locker room for a shower and to change, I'm ready for a big juicy burger and shake from Louie's, the dive restaurant that's very popular in our small town.

"Hey, are you going to Louie's tonight or just hanging out with Kristen?" I ask Steven, as we both finish getting dressed.

"I think we'll hit it up before we ditch everyone to go find someplace quiet, if you know what I mean," he tells me, bouncing his eyebrows up and down at me with a smirk on his face.

"Sounds good, bro. Is Lauren coming out with us?" I ask him.

"Hell if I know. I haven't talked to her since third period. But if she does, keep an eye on her, please. I think Chad's been trying to make a move on her."

My stomach clenches at that thought. Chad better keep

his hands off of her. He's the biggest douche in our school, and his player reputation was well-earned.

We finally file out of the locker room and into the parking lot. It's still pretty full of groups of students milling around as everyone makes plans for the rest of the night. I spot Lauren, leaning against my truck, talking with a few of our mutual friends.

"Hey, good game, guys," Lauren calls out to me and Steven as we approach her. "You guys did great out there."

"Thanks, Ren," I tell her, giving her a one-armed hug as I sling my gear bag into the back of my truck with the other arm.

"Good job, babe," I hear Kristen tell Steven before I hear the smack of lips colliding together.

"Are you coming out with us tonight?" I ask Lauren, quiet enough that only she can hear me.

"Yep. I've been looking forward to it all day," she tells me with that giant smile on her face.

I can't help but break out into my own huge smile.

"I'm glad you'll be there." I squeeze her once more before I drop my hand from her shoulder and let her go.

We end up with a huge group at Louie's, and after finally getting to order, I find a booth that's just being vacated and snag it for us. Lauren follows shortly behind me and sits down to my left, while Steven and Kristen take the bench across from us once they finish ordering.

The entire time we're eating, I'm very aware of every time Lauren and I brush accidentally against each other. A small brush of our hands as we each reach for our drinks at the same time, or our hands grazing each other's when we've rested them on the bench. That time, I linked our pinkies together and squeezed hers, tossing a wink her way when she looked at me with those questioning eyes of hers. Always so full of life, yet still so naive.

Steven and Kristen ditch us, and the atmosphere around us changes. Our simple touches from before, all of a sudden don't feel so innocent.

Lauren turns toward me as I turn to her. No words are spoken between us as we both stare each other down. Our heads slowly start to move closer to each other, almost of their own accord. I reach up a hand to cup her cheek, feeling like I'm in a dream, finally about to kiss the one girl who's always been out of reach to me.

The one girl who I've always wanted but could never have.

With our faces inches apart, our connection is snapped when Steven bangs on the window, effectively breaking the moment between us.

All I can do is laugh. The moment is gone; I just have to hope we get another one like it soon.

Lauren just laughs at her brother's antics and shrugs at me when I turn back to her.

"Let's go!" she suggests, grabbing my hand and pulling me out of the booth behind her.

I let her, not only because I want to keep an eye on her tonight if she ends up at one of the parties about to go down, but because I'd follow this girl anywhere.

5

LAUREN

NOW

I STAND IN THE BEDROOM OF MY GRANDPARENTS' HOUSE where I'll be getting ready today. I look around at all the pictures from my childhood they have on display here in the room. All those amazing memories of time spent here on the farm. Even after they retired and had sold off most of the land, we still spent plenty of time here, making memories that will forever stay with me, that I hope to one day pass down to my own kids.

"Knock, knock." My best friend and maid of honor, Zoey, opens the door and smiles at me. "How are you doing this morning?" she asks, handing me a cup of coffee.

"I'm good. Excited. Nervous. Ready to see Brad."

"Ready to get started on your hair and makeup?"

"As ready as I'm going to get," I tell her as I take a sip of the coffee. I hope the jolt of caffeine helps settle my nerves and this nagging feeling that just won't go away. It's a little unsettling, but I'm sure it's just the nerves taking root.

"Sit down here and I'll get started," Zoey instructs. There are perks to having a best friend who loves both being a girly girl and her makeup. I've never been the girl who was obsessed with it, so I need all the help I can get on what's going to be an important day.

Zoey pulls out her bag of makeup and sets out some items as I get comfortable in the chair she wants me in.

"Did you sleep well?" she asks as she starts by pulling my hair into a bun, so it's out of my face and her way.

"So-so," I tell her honestly. "After everyone turned in last night, I was just feeling so restless. I ended up going outside and sitting in the reception tent. Taking in everything and just thinking about our future."

"Everything okay?"

I haven't told anyone about this nagging feeling, the one where I'm about to make a mistake by marrying Brad.

"Can I tell you something that you promise not to tell anyone?"

This causes her to stop applying the foundation, and she puts down the sponge and looks me in the eye.

"Of course, you know you can always talk to me about anything."

Exhaling, I sit up a little straighter in the chair. I bite my lip, stalling a bit longer, not really sure if I'm ready to share this worry that's been plaguing me for a while now.

"You're scaring me, Ren. What's going on?"

"I've..." I pause, sucking in a deep breath, doing my best to calm my nerves. "I've had this nagging feeling the last couple of weeks, that has progressively gotten worse these last few days. Like I'm about to make the biggest mistake of my life if I marry Brad."

"So, like, cold feet?" Zoey asks.

"I don't think this is just a case of cold feet. I feel it in my bones, almost. When I sat outside last night in the tent, I tried to visualize my life in one, five, hell, even twenty-five years from now, and all I see is Sam next to me. I think I need to call off my wedding. I don't think I can marry Brad."

"Oh, Ren," she says, pulling me into a hug. "Are you sure? Do you want me to go find your mom so that you can talk to her for a bit?"

Tears streak my cheeks as I nod, a million thoughts running through my mind. Today is supposed to be one of the happiest days of my life. One that I will remember forever, tell my kids and my grandchildren about one day. I'm not supposed to be sitting here, crying my eyes out, thinking about one man while I get ready to walk down the aisle toward another.

I hear the creak of the door opening again as my mom rushes inside the room and over to me. She wraps her arms around me, and the small amount of restraint I was holding on to breaks, the flood of tears and hiccupping sobs escaping from me.

"Shhh... shhhh, Ren. Everything's going to be okay, sweetie," my mom tells me, as she does her best to comfort me.

It takes me a few moments to slow the sobs and regain my composure. I accept the tissues Zoey found and is handing to me. I dry my cheeks and blow my nose before looking up at both of them.

"Oh, my darling girl. What's wrong?" my mom asks.

"That's the million-dollar question," I tell her, trying to lighten the mood just a bit. "I'm just worried I'm about to make a mistake."

"It's normal to feel scared before getting married, honey," she tells me. "I was a nervous wreck when I married your father, and look at us now. Thirty-three years later, and we're still madly in love with each other."

"I know, Mom, and I love Brad, I really do. I just can't shake that he's not the one I should be marrying."

"I'll support you in anything you decide, but are you ready to make that call? Do you want to talk to him, maybe see if you can work out some of your fears?"

I suck in a shuddering breath. *Am I ready to face him and possibly break his heart?*

"Isn't it bad luck for me to see him before the ceremony?"

"So what, some people say and think that, but if you're this distraught over the decision, I'd think it'd be best to talk to him. Let him know what you're feeling and why, and come to a decision together."

I take in a few deeper breaths, mulling over what my mom has just suggested. I don't know what to do. I'm at such a loss right now.

"I love Brad, I really do. It would crush him to know that I'm struggling I just don't think I can do that to him right now," I say to the room, stalling as I gather my strength and pull myself together. "I'll be fine. Let's get back to getting ready, and I'll be fine. I'm sure it's just a case of cold feet."

I sit up straighter, wiping my eyes one last time. I'm determined not to think about this nagging feeling again. Today is the happiest day of my life, and I'm going to enjoy it.

6

SAM

NOW

I FINALLY PULL MYSELF OUT OF BED, AND INTO THE SHOWER. My head isn't pounding as bad as I expected it, after drinking my weight in whiskey last night.

My heart can't take much more today, and I'm afraid my liver might not be able to either. I don't know how I'm going to make it through the ceremony today, but I have to be there to support Lauren.

As I step out of the shower, I hear my cell ringing by the bed. I wrap the towel around my waist and quickly shuffle out to grab my phone. As I pick it up, I see Steven's name flash on the screen. I try and answer, but miss it as it rolls over to my voicemail.

I quickly click on his name to call him back, putting the call on speaker. I toss my phone back onto the bed, so I can finish toweling off and pull on some clothes. The wedding isn't until this afternoon, so I don't need to get my suit on this early.

"Good morning," Steven greets me as he answers his phone. "Are you alive this morning?"

I chuckle. "Yeah, I'm alive. Not doing as bad as I thought

I would be, after all the whiskey last night. I just got out of the shower, you want to grab some breakfast?"

"I was calling to ask you the same thing. Meet at the diner in thirty?"

"See ya there, man," I tell him before he hangs up.

After I finish getting ready, I grab my wallet and stuff it in my back pocket. Picking up my phone and keys, I head to the parking lot and jump in my rental to head to the diner.

I beat Steven there, so I grab us a table; what used to be our normal one growing up. The same damn one I almost kissed Lauren in all those years ago.

I pull out the menu, not that I need to read the damn thing. It hasn't changed in the forty-odd years this place has been open.

"Long time, no see, stranger," Betty, one of the waitresses who has worked here as long as I can remember, says to me as she stops at the table.

I smile up at her. "Good to see you, Ms. Betty. How are you doing these days?"

"I'm good, sugar. How are you? In town for Ren's wedding?"

"Sure am, wouldn't miss it for the world." I plaster a smile on my face, hoping I look and sound convincing.

"I always thought you kids would end up together."

You and me both, I think to myself.

"Naw, we never dated. Just one of my best friends."

"You two might have been best friends, but I saw how that girl looked at you all those years. I also noticed how you looked at her when you didn't think anyone watching."

I pale, and swallow hard.

"Got anything good on special today?" I ask, hoping to change the subject.

"Today's breakfast special is the steak and eggs, with hash browns and toast."

"That sounds perfect. I'll take that, with wheat toast and a large glass of OJ. Add on a side of biscuits and gravy while you're at it. I've been craving them lately."

"Coming right up. Will it just be you this morning?"

"No, Steven should be here shortly," I tell her, just as he walks in the door. "Actually, here he is now."

"Mornin', sugar," she calls out to Steven as he takes the few steps over to the table.

"Good morning, Ms. Betty," he greets her, as he leans down to kiss her on the cheek.

"What can I get you this morning?"

"I'll take my normal this morning, with a cup of coffee."

"Coming right up," she says, pivoting around and heading for the kitchen.

"Thanks, Ms. Betty," we both call after her, getting a small wave of her hand as she puts our order ticket in the window of the kitchen.

"So, how was the rest of your night?" Steven asks me a few minutes later, as Betty sets our drinks down on the table in front of us.

"Eh, after we parted ways, I just went back to my room and crashed. I didn't want to be too hungover today. Have you talked to her yet this morning?"

"I haven't, I figured I'd head over to the house once we finish breakfast. Renee is still back at the house with Ethan. She was going to stay home until closer to showtime, to keep him on his normal schedule as much as possible. Do you want to head over to the house with me when we're done here?"

"Maybe. I'll need to head back to the hotel to grab my suit first, at least. I might also just stay away until closer to when the wedding is scheduled to start. I wouldn't want to make an ass of myself by trying to confess my feelings before she walks down the aisle."

Betty arrives then, with our loaded plates, and we both dig right in. The first bite that hits my tongue has me moaning at how excellent the food tastes.

"God, I missed this place," I say between bites. "No place I find can measure up to the food here."

We finish our meals and after settling up with Betty, we both take off. I head for the hotel while Steven heads to his grandparents' house.

After getting back to the hotel, I lie down on the bed and decide a short nap will be the best thing I can do to pass the time. I don't want to do anything stupid today, so staying away from Lauren until it's time to arrive for the ceremony will be for the best. It isn't just her dad that will be giving her away today. The feeling of my heart being ripped from my chest is settling in, and I'm still not sure how I'm going to make it through today without standing up to object.

Sam

17 years old

"HEY, SAM! WAIT UP!" I HEAR LAUREN CALL TO ME FROM down the senior hall. I stop walking and turn in her direction. The smile filling her face brings one to my own. She's always been a bubbly person, but I can tell she has something to tell me.

"What's got you all giddy, Ren?" I ask as she stops in front of me, bouncing on the balls of her feet, her curly blonde hair bouncing all around her face.

"I got, not one, but *two* letters today!" she practically shouts in my face, the excitement filling her voice.

"From where?" I ask, knowing exactly what she's referring to. It's the time of year when all of us seniors are awaiting our acceptance letters from the colleges we've applied to.

"University of Kentucky and Ohio State!" she exclaims.

"That's so awesome! Do you know which one you want to pick?" I ask her as we start walking toward the parking lot.

"I'm leaning towards staying here and going to UK. That way, I not only save by paying in-state tuition, but I can also still live at home and save the cost of living in the dorms. I know I'll miss out on the experience of the dorms, but I want to focus on my classes and schoolwork more than I want that."

"I'm happy for you, Ren." I sling my arm around her shoulders and pull her into my side.

"Plus, if I stayed and go to UK, I'll get to see you all the time."

I'd already signed a letter of intent and accepted a full-ride scholarship to play football with the University of Kentucky earlier this year.

"I'll be living on campus, so you can always come visit me in the football dorms." I pause. "Actually, maybe you won't be able to come visit me in the dorms. I don't want all those bastards thinking they can try and date you," I tease.

"Very funny, Sam. You and Steven can't keep all the guys away from me forever. I'm a big girl, I can decide when and who I want to date," she huffs at me.

So it appears she's caught on that we've pretty much threatened every guy in our class, and maybe even the junior class, that they will answer to not just one of us, but both of us, if any of them even attempt to ask her out. No one is good enough for her.

No one ever will be, in my eyes.

Sam
Now

I'm startled awake from my short snooze by the alarm on my phone going off. I started dreaming about Lauren and me in high school and the day came back to me as if I'd just lived it today. The excitement she possessed that day her acceptance letters arrived still brought a smile to my face.

I roll out of bed and after a quick stop in the bathroom, I pull out my black suit to get ready for Lauren's big day.

Before I leave my room, I slip my flask filled with whiskey in my inner suit pocket. I have a feeling it's the only way I'm going to make it through, since I can't just skip out and not attend the wedding of my best friend, the woman who I've loved for years.

I pull up to the farmhouse, making sure to park my rental car off to the side, in a place I hope I don't end up being blocked in. That's all I need, to want to make a quick exit and end up trapped by some asshole. After pulling out the gift I picked up yesterday from one of the stores where Lauren was registered, I make my way toward the tent set up in the back. I find the gift table and set down the box that's filled with some kitchen items. Lauren always loved to bake, so I figured she'd enjoy some things to fill her own kitchen to carry on the tradition.

Pictures from both Lauren and Brad's childhoods are

framed and set out all around the tables. I stop, looking over all the memories. I only pay attention to the ones of Lauren; the memories that some of the images bring back fill me with even more nostalgia of the past and how close we used to be.

We stayed close throughout college. With both of us attending UK all four years of college, Lauren was always there cheering me on at the home football games, and I was still there, doing my best to scare off all the guys that were drawn to her. Unfortunately for me, she kept Brad to herself until after they started dating. I'll never forget how pissy she got with Steven and me, the day she introduced him to us and we both about lost it on the guy.

———

Sam
20 years old

Ren: Hey, you busy tonight?

Sam: Nope, you want to meet up for dinner? I feel like I haven't seen you in weeks.

Ren: Yes! I know, sorry about that. These classes have been kicking my butt this semester. But if it's any consolation, I miss you.

Sam: Good to know, Ren. Wouldn't want you to forget about me. 😊

Ren: Like I could ever! Does Goodfellas Pizzeria sound okay to you? I've also texted Steven to see if he can join us.

Sam: Sure. What time?

Ren: Is 5:30 too early?

Sam: That works for me. See ya then.

I ARRIVED AT THE RESTAURANT A FEW MINUTES BEFORE I'M supposed to meet Lauren and Steven for dinner. As I walk up, I notice Lauren standing at the hostess stand, putting her name on the list, I'm sure. As I get closer, she steps to the side and right into the arms of some guy.

What the fuck.

She pushes up on her toes and plants a kiss right on this dude's lips. My steps falter and I come to a stop, taking it all in and hoping my eyes are playing tricks on me. I look around, waiting for Steven to pop out and tell me it's all a prank. Steven is nowhere to be found, but Lauren turns her head in my direction and catches me watching her.

"Sam!" she eagerly greets me as she closes the distance between the two of us. "I'm so glad you made it. I wanted to introduce you to my boyfriend, Brad."

Boyfriend. What the ever-loving-fuck.

"Your what?" I almost spit out at her as I return the hug she's got me wrapped up in.

"Boyfriend," she says, smiling up at me, then tugs me toward the guy who's still standing in the same spot she left him.

I size him up as we approach. I can't say that I've ever met the guy, only seen him around campus.

"Brad, Sam. Sam, Brad." She introduces us to each other. "As I've told you many times, Sam and I grew up together. Steven, Sam, and I have been best friends since my family moved in across the street from his family."

"Nice to meet you, man. Thanks for always looking out for my girl. She speaks highly of you," Brad says, as he sticks his hand out to shake mine.

My girl, asshole. I accept his hand, making sure to grip his as firmly as I can, to make him take note of my strength and maybe catch on that I'll hurt him if he hurts Lauren.

"Lauren, party of four," the hostess calls out.

"Right here," she calls back as we turn in her direction. We all follow the hostess to a booth in the back, accepting the menus she hands us after we each take a seat.

Lauren lets Brad into the booth first and she takes the seat next to him. I slide into the booth across from her and stay so I'm sitting across from her and not Brad.

"What time is Steven coming?" I ask, needing to fill the silence and wanting to know how long I have to be around this guy without backup.

"He should be here any minute. I'll text him now, to let him know we have a booth and to just head back to us," she says, pulling out her cell and shooting off a text to her brother. A reply text sounds almost instantly. "He should be here in just a few minutes, he says. Just a few blocks away."

"Sounds good," I tell her as I look over the menu.

"Good evening, I'm Kate, and I'll be your server tonight. Can I start you out with something to drink? Maybe an appetizer?"

"I'll have an iced tea, please," Brad tells her.

"I'll take a lemonade," Ren says, before returning her attention to the menu.

"And for you?" she asks, flashing me a smile that brings out her dimples.

"Just water for now. Thanks, Kate." I toss her a wink, and she blushes before walking away to fill our drink order. I glance over at Lauren and see a look pass over her face, but it disappears so quickly, I wonder if I imagined it.

"Oh, he's here," Lauren says, standing from the booth and taking a few steps toward her brother.

"Hey, Ren," Steven says, his gaze landing on Brad and then bouncing to me with a questioning look on his face. I just answer by shrugging my shoulders.

"Steven, I wanted to introduce you to someone," she tells him as they both step up to the table. "Steven, this is Brad. Brad, this is my brother, Steven. Brad and I have been dating for about a month now."

I can almost see the steam coming out of Steven's ears when Ren mentions she's been dating this guy for a fucking month.

"A month, Ren? Really. What the fuck. We don't keep things from each other," Steven grits out.

"Well, with the caveman thing going on between the two of you, I had to keep this from you if I ever wanted to start dating someone serious," she tells him, steeling her spine and standing up to him.

Okay, so maybe we've overdone the protection detail, but fuck, if this didn't hit me out of thin air.

"Nice to meet you," Brad pipes up, sticking his hand out for Steven to shake.

From the small wince on Brad's face, I'm guessing Steven did as I did and squeezed just a tad bit hard when they shook hands.

Lauren returns to her place next to Brad, and I slide over in the booth so that Steven can slip in next to me.

"So, anything else new that you haven't told me about?" Steven asks Lauren as he settles in next to me.

"Nope," she tells him, popping the P as she does so.

I don't miss the way Brad slips his arm around her, pulling her slightly closer to his side as she places her hand on what I'm assuming is his leg. I draw in a deep breath, not liking this display in front of me at all. I need to get out of here, or some whiskey, stat. Since I can't make a quick exit, whiskey it'll be.

"Why don't I believe you?" Steven volleys back at her, a

serious look on his face. He's accepting this information just about as well as I am.

"I don't know, but you have to remember that I'm an adult and can make my own decisions. You can knock off the 'big brother' card. You're only two minutes older than me and that stick is getting a little old. I don't need you protecting me for the rest of my life. I just need you to be happy for me and trust my judgment. Okay?"

Fuck. She's right. We do need to trust her. Doesn't mean we have to like it, but it does mean that we need to let her live her life.

"Sorry, Ren," Steven grumbles next to me. "When you put it like that, it makes me feel like a dick."

"I still love you, but tame down the alpha male-protective brother routine just a few notches. Okay? You'll be the first person I call if I need something, I promise."

WE MAKE IT THROUGH DINNER WITH LAUREN AND BRAD, whiskey not even necessary. The guy wasn't that bad, and it was apparent that they liked each other equally. As much as I hated to admit it, Lauren deserved to find someone to love her and cherish her. I just wish it could be me. No matter who got that right, the guy would never be good enough for her in my eyes—me included.

When our waitress brings back our checks to sign, I noticed she left me her number on the back of mine. She did her best to flirt with me the few times she stopped at the table, and I didn't mind one bit. She's cute but feisty, so I make sure to tuck the receipt in my wallet when I slide my card back in and make a mental note to text her later tonight to set up a date.

7

LAUREN

NOW

I PEEK OUT THE WINDOW OVERLOOKING MY GRANDPARENTS' backyard, where we have the ceremony spot all set up. I watch as Brad and my family and friends gather around, talking and starting to fill in the chairs. It's almost time for me to make my way downstairs.

As I'm watching out the window, I catch a glimpse of Sam. He looks so good in his black suit. I only got to talk to him for a few minutes last night, so I'm hopeful we can catch up more tonight at the reception.

The uneven feelings I was experiencing this morning subsided, and thankfully aren't returning, even after seeing him.

A knock on the door draws my attention away from the window as I turn to see who's coming in to check on me.

"Hey, sweetheart." My dad opens the door and walks into the room. "You look beautiful," he tells me, choking back the emotion that's threatening to spill out.

"Thank you."

"You ready to get this show on the road? Grandpa's all set and ready to marry you off," he says with a chuckle.

My parents have done everything to make this wedding my dream. From the small country feel, to the venue being on my grandparents' property. I've always wanted my grandfather to marry me, as well, and I'm just grateful he's still healthy and able to do so. The last touch I've always dreamed about having at my wedding was magnolia flowers everywhere. They've always been my favorite flower, and my mom made sure they were a big part of the decorations for today.

"As ready as I'm going to get." I smile up at him as I slip my arm through his and let him lead me out the door, down the stairs to my future.

My mom and Zoey meet us at the bottom of the staircase, smiles filling their faces.

"You look stunning," my mom tells me again. "We're all set and ready for you outside."

"I'm ready."

"Okay then, I'll head out and get things started."

My mom gives me one last hug before turning to make her way outside. Zoey walks around me, fixing the back of my dress and handing me my flowers.

"You good?" she asks.

"I'm good," I reply, squeezing her hands.

"Then let's get you married!" She grabs her own bouquet and steps outside to walk down the aisle before me.

"It looks like it's our turn, baby girl," my dad tells me.

We step outside, and I can somewhat see the front area where Brad is standing. He looks so handsome up there in his tux. Tears prick my eyes as we walk toward the back of the aisle. I seek out my brother first, locking eyes with him as he gives me a large smile. Next to him is my sister-in-law, Renee, with my nephew in her arms. I give them a watery smile as I search the crowd for Sam, but I can't find him. I falter, wondering where he could be. I saw him from the window, so I know he's here somewhere.

Sam
Now

AFTER I FINISHED LOOKING AT THE PICTURES SET OUT AND getting lost in the memory of when Lauren first introduced us to Brad, I wander toward the seating area to find Steven.

I bump into a few people I haven't seen in years, making small talk as we catch up. I keep my eyes open for Steven and once I finally find him, I excuse myself to head his way.

Just as I approach him, Renee is handing over the baby to him, having just arrived herself.

"Hey, Sam," she says to me as I stop next to them. I lean down to give her a hug and kiss on the cheek.

"Good to see you. This guy taking good care of you?" I ask, motioning toward Steven.

"Only the best," she says, smiling up at her husband.

The love these two have for each other is almost contagious. Steven really lucked out when he met Renee, and is one lucky bastard that she's willing to put up with him. They met in college and got married just after graduation. That was a few years ago now, and they are still just as happy as they were the day they said "I do".

"Good to hear. If that changes, you just call me, and I'll knock some sense into him for you," I tell her, knowing full well that would never happen. Steven practically worships the ground she walks on.

"Don't worry one bit, I know how to keep my woman

satisfied." Steven smirks and winks at his wife, who's blushing now.

"Are you going to sit with us?" Renee asks me.

"Ah, I think I'll just find a place in the back," I tell her as my stomach flops and the dread sets in again.

"You going to make it through okay?" Steven asks me.

"Hope so. Just don't let me stand up and object."

"Kinda hard to do if you're hiding out in the back."

Sighing, I rub the back of my neck and blow out a breath. "Yeah, I know. I just don't think I can sit up front with you guys. I don't need to be that close to the action. I don't need to actually hear her pledge her life to him."

Steven pats me on the back. "Whatever you think will get you through, I'll support you, man."

"Thanks. Guess it's time to go find a seat. Looks like they are ready to start," I tell them.

"That's my cue then, to go get ready to escort Mom down the aisle." Steven hands baby Ethan to Renee before he leans down and kisses her. "Love you," he says to her before walking away.

I follow him down the aisle, stopping at the last row of chairs. "See you when this is over. We'll grab a drink together as soon as the bar opens up," Steven tells me before he continues to the house to find his mom.

I take a seat, the farthest one from the center aisle. As the seats around me fill in, the gripping feeling takes hold of me. I don't know that I can stay here and watch this happen.

I've been in love with Lauren since we were kids. It feels like my heart is about to be torn out of my chest, and I'm not sure that I can put myself through that. I reach into the inside pocket of my suit jacket and take out the flask, quickly taking a swig. The burn of the whiskey as it slides down my throat shocks my system just enough.

I bolt from my seat and head to my car. I can't make myself sit through this. I can't trust that I won't make a fool of myself and hurt Lauren by standing up when her grandfather asks if anyone objects the marriage.

Once in my car, I suck in a deep breath and lay my head against the headrest, closing my eyes. Once I've got my nerves calmed down, I start the car, hoping that no one notices me escaping. I drive away slowly and head to the diner. I don't know why I head there, but it's where I end up.

"What are you doing here? Shouldn't you be at the wedding that's about to start?" Betty asks me as I take a seat at the same booth where Steven and I sat earlier.

"I couldn't do it, Ms. Betty. I tried. I couldn't make an ass of myself and hurt Lauren by objecting, so I just left."

"All right, well, I guess leaving was for the best then. Can I get you anything?"

"Just a coffee for now would be great," I tell her as I pull out my phone.

Sam: I couldn't do it, man. I left. I'm down at the diner.

I figured it was best to let Steven know I bolted and not to look for me. I might slip back in once the ceremony is over and the reception has started.

Ms. Betty drops off the cup of coffee, patting my back before she walks away to tend to her other tables. I pull out the flask from my pocket again, adding a little to my coffee.

I sit there, the heaviness of the day washing over me. I slowly drink my coffee, and just watch the other diners as I sit here, wallowing.

I'm not sure how much time has passed, but something catches my eye out the window. When I look up, Lauren is standing in front of me, tears tracking down her face. I jump

34

out of the booth as fast as I can, and am out the door and standing in front of her within seconds.

"W-what are you doing here?" I ask her as I pull her into my arms.

"I couldn't go through with it. I couldn't marry him when I'm in love with someone else," she tells me, pulling me tighter against her as she buries her face in the crook of my neck.

Holy shit, what does this mean? Who in the hell could she be in love with?

I hold her tight against me, shushing her as I rub her back.

Her crying grows quiet and as I feel her take in a few deep breaths, I pull back from her slightly so that I can look at her. I bring a hand up to cup her face, wiping at the last few tears with the pad of my thumb.

"Tell me what happened."

She sucks in a shaky breath, calming herself. "Can we go in and sit down first?"

"Oh, yes, absolutely." I escort her inside the diner and to my booth.

She slides in on the same side I was sitting on, and pats the seat, silently asking me to sit next to her. I comply, and settle in next to her, leaving a few inches between the two of us.

She fumbles, rubbing her hands together, obviously thinking over what she's about to tell me. I sit, doing my best to keep patient, while my mind is running crazy. I feel my phone vibrating in my pocket and pull it out to see a text from Steven.

Steven: Did Lauren come find you? She bolted from the wedding.

Sam: Yes, she just got here a few seconds ago. I'll text you later.

Steven: Okay, just checking as she didn't say much to any of us before she bolted. I just wanted to make sure she was ok.

I slip my phone back in my pocket, turning my attention back to her.

"That was Steven, just checking to see if I knew where you were. He's worried about you."

"I know," she whispers. "I kinda bolted, didn't know where I was going. Just knew I needed to get away from there."

"Ready to tell me what made you leave?"

She sucks in another deep breath, turning as much as she can in the booth toward me. Her wedding dress, thankfully, isn't a huge puffy one, so it doesn't take up much of the space between us.

"The past few months I've had this feeling like something wasn't right, like I was about to make a mistake. The feeling intensified over the last few days and I tried to push it aside, thinking it was normal wedding jitters. Last night, after the rehearsal and after everyone turned in, I went and sat in the reception tent, trying to decipher all the thoughts running through my head. I couldn't shake the feeling. As I sat there, thinking about the past and the future, all I could see was you."

Lauren pauses, wiping away a tear that's sliding down her face.

"I tossed and turned all night and this morning, and woke up with the feeling even stronger. I had a big meltdown this morning before I started getting ready. Zoey and Mom tried to get me to call off the wedding, or at least talk to Brad, but I didn't want to do that to him. I pushed forward with getting ready and by the time the ceremony was to start, I was feeling better. When Dad and I arrived at the back of the aisle, I looked for you, but couldn't find you. I knew you were there, as I'd seen you from the window when I was still upstairs. I looked everywhere and when I couldn't find you, my heart sank. By then, Dad and I had started walking down the aisle, and when we reached the front, I knew I couldn't go through with it. I couldn't marry Brad when I was in love with you."

Holy shit, she's in love with me?

"Y-y-you're in love with me?" I stutter, reaching out to cup her face.

"Yes," she says, a smile filling her face.

The weight that had been on my shoulders immediately lifts as I bring my forehead to Lauren's. "That's pretty fucking incredible, since I've been in love with you for years, Ren."

Her smile grows bigger, if that's even possible. Her eyes sparkle as she shifts and brushes her lips across my cheek.

"Can we get out of here?" she asks, pulling away from me.

"Sure, where did you want to go?"

"You have a hotel room, right?"

"Yes."

"I think we have lots to discuss, and then I'll need to make an appearance back at the farm, but I'd like to wait a little while before heading back. I'd like for all the guests to have time to leave before I return."

"That's probably a good plan. Have you talked to Brad yet?"

"Not besides when I told him I couldn't do this and apologized before leaving him at the alter. I should probably find him and talk to him, unless he doesn't want to talk to me, which I wouldn't blame him for, if that was the case."

I toss a five on the table and wave to Ms. Betty, whose eyebrows are almost in her hairline as she takes in Lauren and me leaving. I lead Lauren outside, stopping between my car and the one she drove here.

"Did you want to drive yourself, or ride with me?"

"I should probably drive myself, that way I can take Mom her car when I'm ready to head back."

"Sounds good, I'm just staying down at the Marriott. I'll meet you there in a few."

I open the driver's side door for her, holding it until she's settled, and then close it for her. I quickly walk around the front of my car and jump in. I pull my seatbelt on as I start the car, and immediately put it in reverse so I can get on the road.

8

LAUREN

I look over the guests again, searching for Sam. Where the hell could he be? Dad squeezes my hand as we start to walk down the aisle.

"Everything okay, sweetheart?" Dad asks, leaning down.

All I can do is give him a watery half-smile. I don't even know if everything is okay. The sinking feeling has returned, and I don't think I can go through with this. As we near the end of the aisle, where Brad is standing, waiting on me, I falter more. I lock eyes with my brother, hoping he can ground me. But all I'm met with is a concerned look. I can tell he knows something is wrong.

I swing my gaze back to the altar and lock eyes with Zoey. She gives me a worried look as well, mouthing "Everything okay?" All I can do is slightly shake my head no at her. I break eye contact with her and bring my focus to Brad. He's standing there, watching me intently. His face quickly morphs from a smile to a look of dread.

Dad and I reach the front and before my grandfather can say anything, I reach for Brad's hands. I finally speak, talking only loud enough that the few of us standing there can hear.

"I'm so sorry, but I can't do this. You deserve better. I'll explain everything later, but for now, I need to go," I say, dropping Brad's hands, and I hurry back down the aisle. I quickly run inside my grandparents' house, entering into the kitchen. I see my mom's keys on the counter and I grab them, then run back outside, praying her car isn't blocked in. I find it quickly and send up a quick prayer that I can easily maneuver it out of the driveway.

I head straight for the diner. It was one of the places we'd always gone, and I had a feeling it was where I'd find Sam. I need to get to him and tell him that I love him. I can't keep it to myself anymore. I've loved that man since we were kids, and I just can't keep that to myself any longer.

I pull up in front of the diner and can see him sitting in our booth. Front and center, next to the big front window. I sit there for a moment, taking in his defeated form. I can tell something's bothering him, and I can only hope it has something to do with me and marrying Brad.

I suck in a deep breath, steeling my nerves as I open the car door and climb out. I walk up to the diner, stopping outside the window. It only takes a few seconds for Sam to look out and see me standing there in front of him, tears sliding down my cheeks.

The shocked look on his face pulls a laugh from my chest. I just shrug my shoulders at him as he quickly gets up and comes running outside.

"W-what are you doing here?" he asks, pulling me into his arms as soon as he reaches me.

"I couldn't go through with it. I couldn't marry him when I'm in love with someone else," I tell him as I pull him tighter against me, burying my face in the crook of his neck.

After awhile, we head back inside the diner and I tell him what happened. The shock is starting to wear off, and I need to get out of here and somewhere I can relax for a little while as the dust settles.

"Can we get out of here?" I finally ask.

"Sure, where did you want to go?"

"You have a hotel room, right?" I ask, fairly sure he isn't crashing at Steven and Renee's house.

"Yes."

"I think we have lots to discuss, and then I'll need to make an appearance back at the farm, but I'd like to wait a little while before heading back. I'd like for all the guests to have time to leave before I return."

We leave the diner and I follow Sam to his hotel just a few miles away. Thankfully, we don't see anyone we know as we walk into the hotel and to his room. The people we do see probably think we just got married and are sneaking off to our hotel room. Little do they know, I just left my groom at the altar.

We make it into his room and I collapse on the bed.

"Can I get you anything? Wine, whiskey, tequila?" he offers.

"You wouldn't happen to have something I can change into, would you?" My dress was starting to annoy me, and I was feeling a little weird still dressed in it. I wasn't getting married today.

"I'm sure I can find you something, I can't guarantee you won't be swimming in it," he says, going over to his suitcase and pulling out a t-shirt and a pair of basketball shorts. He turns back around and hands them to me.

"Thank you," I whisper as I grab them from him and walk to the bathroom.

I set the clothes on the counter and step back into the room.

"Two things. One, do you mind if I take a shower? And two, can you please unzip me?" I ask him, my cheeks burning with embarrassment.

I can see his Adam's apple move as he swallows hard. "Yeah, sure," he says, stepping closer to me. The feel of his fingertips touching my back is like fire against my skin.

He lowers the zipper, tooth by tooth. It feels like he's purposely torturing me by lowering it so slowly. I reach up and hold the front of my dress so that it doesn't fall to the floor once he's done. He's already going to get an eyeful from the back and be able to see that I only have on some skimpy wedding lingerie.

He finally reaches the bottom of the zipper and his hands drop from my body. "Thank you," I murmur again over my shoulder as I force myself to step away from him and back into the bathroom. I shut the door behind me and sink back against it. My heart pounds, and my skin is still burning from his touch.

I step out of my dress, hanging it up on the hook that's on the back of the door. I turn on the shower, giving it a little time to warm up. In the meantime, I strip out of my strapless bra and thong. I look in the mirror as I start to take out the pins holding my hair up and remove the magnolia flowers that Zoey had tucked in at the last minute, setting them on the counter.

After I finally get all the pins out, I step under the water and let it wash away the day. I can feel the weight from the dread I'd been feeling fall away as the water washes down my body. Unfortunately, it's replaced with regret and sadness. Regret that I let it get this far. Sadness for Brad that I left him at the altar. *God, that was a bitch move. He probably hates me.* No matter how right it was to not marry him, I still loved him, even if I wasn't *in* love with him. He didn't deserve that, and I should have talked with him this morning.

I stand under the water until my skin is well past wrinkled. I quickly wash my hair with the hotel's shampoo, and then shut off the water as it starts to run a bit cold.

I dry off and wrap my hair up in one of the towels, then put my bra and thong back on, as well as the t-shirt and shorts Sam gave me. Both are nearly falling off me, but it's better than the alternative. Thankfully, the shorts have a drawstring, so I'm able to tie them tight enough to stay up. I also tie the t-shirt on my left hip to keep it from swallowing me whole.

Stepping out of the bathroom, I hear Sam talking and quickly realize he's on his phone. It's then that I realize I don't have my cell, and my family is probably freaking out about where I ran off to.

"Yeah, we'll head back that way soon. She just got out of the shower and is doing okay. She just wanted to give enough time for people to clear out. She doesn't really want to have to face everyone right now," I hear him telling whoever he's talking to.

I give him a small smile and a nod of appreciation as he looks at me from across the room.

"Thank you," I tell him as he sets his phone on the small table next to him. "And I'm sorry for putting you in the middle of all of this."

"You don't have anything to apologize to me about. I'd do anything for you, Ren. You know that, right?"

His sincerity chokes me up and I have a hard time keeping the tears at bay.

"Come here," he rasps out as he stands from the chair he

was in. It's then I notice he's lost the tie and jacket, and the top few buttons of his dress shirt have been unbuttoned. I walk over to him, directly into his open arms as he wraps me into a hug.

"I need you to promise me something. I need to know that no matter what comes of this, that you will always tell me what you're thinking and how you feel. No more of this hiding things from each other. I know we have a lot to talk about and figure out, but I want you to know that my love for you will *never* change. You're still one of my best friends on this earth and I don't want to lose that. It's killed me these last handful of years, not being as close as we were growing up. I'll shoulder some of the blame for that, as I purposefully stayed away because it killed me to see you with him."

"I promise," I tell him.

"Ready to head back? Steven said everyone has cleared out, it's just your immediate family left. He said Brad even left with his parents. Just wants you to call him later. They realized pretty quickly that you didn't have your cell with you, so he gave up trying to call you."

"Yeah, might as well get it over with."

9

SAM

I escort Lauren out to the parking lot and into her mom's car, then follow her back to her grandparents' house. As soon as I park, I shut off my car and jump out so that I can get to Lauren's door and open it for her. I want to be next to her when she enters the house, so she feels my support if she needs it.

Neither of us say anything to each other as we walk the few feet up to the door. Lauren stops at the top step and before reaching out for the handle, she takes in a deep breath. I place my hand at the small of her back, hoping my strength passes through to her.

A moment later, she's opening the door and we both walk into the house. We can hear voices coming from the kitchen, so we head in that direction.

Ryan is facing the doorway we walk through, so he sees us first.

"Hi, baby girl. How are you holding up?" he asks his daughter as he steps toward her to pull her into his arms.

"Okay," she says on a shaky breath.

"Want to talk about it?"

"Not really. I think I need to talk to Brad first. It's the least I can do."

"Okay. We're here when you're ready." He places a kiss on the top of her head.

She breaks from his arms and makes the rounds, getting hugs from the rest of her family, and Steven steps up next to me. A raised eyebrow is all I get from him, and his look asks, "What the fuck is going on?"

I just shake my head and mouth, "Later" to him. He gets the hint and doesn't try and push me for anything else at the moment. Not that I have much to tell him yet. He knows how I feel and where I stand when it comes to Lauren. Hell, he's tried to push me into telling her many times over the years.

God, I should have listened to him.

Lauren leaves the room and I hear her head up the stairs to the bedrooms. She returns a few minutes later, changed into a pair of jeans and a shirt of her own, her cell gripped tightly in her hand.

"I'm going to go meet Brad, I'll be back in a while," she announces to the room.

"Do you want anyone to go with you?" her mom asks.

"No, this is something I need to do on my own, and I'm not sure how long I'll be. But I have my phone now, so text me if you need me," she says, before walking out of the kitchen, and I hear the front door close a few moments later.

10

LAUREN

I texted Brad as soon as I got upstairs and to my phone. He'd called it a few times, and sent me no fewer than ten text messages ranging from concern to pissed off and every emotion in between. I don't fault him one bit for any of them. I'd probably have done the same thing had the positions been reversed.

He answered my text immediately and agreed to meet me at the hotel we'd reserved a room at for tonight.

The drive over to the hotel is quiet as I think of everything I need to tell him. I keep the radio off, not wanting the noise right now. It feels so weird to be in this situation. The weight's been lifted, except a new weight has replaced it, due to the guilt of what I did to Brad.

I pull up to the hotel a few minutes later, parking near the side entrance he said he'd meet me by. I see him standing next to it, a glum expression on his face.

I timidly walk up to him, my hands fidgeting with my keys and phone.

"Hi," I say as I stop directly in front of him.

"Hi," he replies on a sigh.

We both stand there in slightly uncomfortable silence.

"Shall we go in and talk?" I ask quietly.

"Yeah, sure." He has a defeated look on his face.

I follow him up the stairs and down the hall to the hotel room that was supposed to be our honeymoon suite. I walk in and see the champagne chilling in the ice bucket and the plate of chocolate-covered strawberries on the desk. Looking around, my gaze falls to the floor, and I see the remnants of some rose petals that were probably on the bed, that Brad has already removed.

I take a seat on one of the chairs next to the window as Brad stays standing next to the king-sized bed.

"I'm sorry," I finally say, breaking the silence. "I really want you to know that. I never meant for it to happen. I should have told you earlier that I was having second thoughts."

Brad blows out an audible breath, almost chuckling, but not in a funny way at all. "That would have been nice. Anything would have been better than you ditching me at the altar." He rubs his face with his hand, squeezing the bridge of his nose, as if he's willing a tension headache away.

"Can you tell me why? What changed?" he asks.

I let out the breath I'd been holding and dive headfirst, wanting to get everything out.

"A few months ago, I started having this nagging feeling, like something wasn't right. It only bothered me a few times, and I just figured it was normal wedding jitters. I knew I loved you, and that you loved me, so I just pushed it away, and things would be fine for a while. As we got closer to today, the feeling started coming more frequently and wasn't as easy to push out of my mind.

"Last night, I sat out in the reception tent after everyone

had gone to bed, pondering if I should call off the wedding. I hardly slept last night, constantly tossing and turning. Then, this morning, before I got ready, Zoey realized something was wrong, and tried to get me to talk to you, but I didn't want to hurt you. So, once again, I pushed the feeling aside and went forward with getting ready. I was doing fine until I reached the aisle and it all fell apart from there. I felt like I could hardly breathe, like I was about to make a huge mistake, not only for me but for you, too."

"But why? Is it me? Did I not show you my love enough?" he asks, running his hands through his hair as he tries to understand what went wrong. How we ended up in this position of me leaving him standing at the altar. It isn't like we rushed this decision. Hell, we dated for six years before getting engaged, and our engagement lasted another year and a half. We didn't even live together until we'd graduated college and had been dating for a few years.

"It wasn't you. I promise. And I'm not trying to feed you the 'it's not you, it's me' bullshit. And, of course, you loved me and showed that to me. But I can't stop the feeling that I'm in love with someone else and have been for most of my life. I can't stop feeling like I was doing you a disservice by moving forward with marrying you. It wasn't fair to me, and it definitely wasn't fair to you."

"It's Sam, isn't it?" he questions quietly, the finality of our situation, our relationship, the past eight years together, just done.

"Yes," I answer him honestly.

"I should have known. Does he know?"

"Yes. When I left the ceremony, I went and found him. When I couldn't find him in the audience, I knew he'd left, as I'd seen him earlier from the window, mingling amongst the guests. I found him at the diner. We've only talked enough that he knows I left you at the altar. But I felt like you deserved to hear it from me first, before anyone else."

"I had a feeling that first time you introduced me to him that something was off. It always stayed in the back of my mind, but neither of you ever flirted or did anything to make me think that the feelings were mutual. But I could always tell that he held a torch for you. How long have you been in love with him?"

"Since I was nine years old, if I'm being honest. But in reality, probably since I was sixteen. Only once did we ever almost kiss, but that was interrupted, and the moment never came again. I wished for years that he would see me as more than his best friend or his best friend's sister. When nothing ever happened, I gave up and decided to move on with my life and start dating. Shortly after that, you asked me out again and I finally said yes."

"I was so pumped that you finally gave in to me," he says, a small smile cracking his lips.

"We had some great times together, and I'm sorry I couldn't love you better," I tell him, looking down at my hands sitting in my lap. It's then I notice my engagement ring is still on my left hand. I slip it off, a tear sliding down my cheek at the finality of my relationship with Brad. I hold my hand out to him, depositing the ring in his hand. "It doesn't feel right for me to keep this."

"Yeah, thanks," he says, pocketing the ring. He'd taken his grandmother's ring and used the diamonds from it to have mine designed. Her ring was cracked and not able to be fixed, so making a new ring from it was the only option. I loved what he'd designed, and would have cherished it had we gotten married, but it was the least I could do to return it to him.

"So, what do we want to do about the condo?" he asks, finally taking a seat in the chair across from me.

"I'm not going to fight you, so I can move out if you don't want to move. I'll even pay my half of the rent for the next few months if you need me to." I'm thankful we put off buying a place of our own for a few years. We weren't sure if Brad's job was going to transfer him in the near future, so we figured it was best to wait to buy.

"You don't have to do that, Ren. You know I can afford it on my own."

"Thank you. I guess I'll come over in the next few days, and pack up my stuff and move it into my parents' garage for now, until I can find an apartment of my own. Maybe when I come over, we can figure out how to split up our stuff, as well as our joint bank account."

"Yeah, that works. I'm off for the next ten days, so just text me and we can set up a time," he tells me, trying to keep the hurt from his voice. I know he's upset, and I'm so grateful he is being so understanding. I don't know that I'd have been able to show this much grace to him had the tables been turned.

With the air between us cleared, or as cleared as it's going to get for now, I stand to leave.

"I just wanted to say I'm sorry again. I never meant to hurt you." A tear slips down my cheek.

He stands, pulling me into his arms, comforting me as if I didn't just finish breaking his heart.

"I know. And as much as this day sucked, I'm sure one day I'll be thankful that you listened to your heart. I'd rather be left at the altar, than get a few months or years down the road and go through a messy divorce."

"Thank you for being so understanding. Someone is out there that is going to make you a happy man and she's one lucky lady. I truly hope you find happiness," I tell him sincerely before walking out of the hotel room.

When I make it down to the car, I sit back in the driver's seat in the silence. It's only just after six, but it feels like it should be after midnight already. I start the car and drive back toward my grandparents' house. I need some food and a bed after the emotional day I've had. Everything else can wait to be dealt with until tomorrow.

11

SAM

After Lauren left, it went from complete silence to everyone talking at once. I stood there as everyone volleyed questions at no one in particular and some at me. I know this family—hell, I've been an honorary member of it for the past nineteen years—and was just as confused as they were over the events from today.

"Listen," I call out over everyone, causing them all to stop talking and listen to what I have to say. "She only talked to me a little bit this afternoon, so I don't know much. She mainly stayed quiet and wanted a place away from everyone while the house emptied out and she could gather her thoughts. She was adamant that she talk to Brad first. I'm not going to tell you what little she told me already, as that's for her to share when she feels ready.

"Once she found me at the diner, I took her back to my hotel, where she took a shower and changed out of her dress, and then we came here. So, as I said, I don't have much more information than that. I'm sure once she returns from talking to Brad, she'll share with you what happened and why she did what she did."

"I knew she was having some second thoughts this morning," Debra says, breaking the silence. "We talked through some of her anxiety and she thought she'd worked through it all. I'm guessing that didn't work and it caused her to run."

Everyone mulls over what Debra has just said, but before anyone says anything else, we hear the front door open and footsteps fill the hall.

"Hi." Lauren's voice fills the kitchen as everyone turns to look at her. She looks worn out and emotionally exhausted. I'm sure the day has taken a toll on her. I'd love nothing more than to whisk her away from here for the night; hell, maybe the next few days. Zoey steps forward and wraps her in a hug, trying to offer her some comfort she obviously needs right now.

"How'd it go?" Steven asks her.

"As good as I could have expected, he was actually really understanding," she says "Mom, do we have anything I can eat? I'm starving and am starting to get shaky."

"Of course, sweetie. I can warm you up a plate of food from the reception food or make you a sandwich, what would you prefer?"

"A plate would be fine." Lauren moves further into the kitchen, grabbing a glass from the cabinet and filling it with some ice and water from the fridge before taking a seat at the table.

Debra brings the plate over and sets it in front of her, handing her some silverware to go along with it. "Eat up, sweetie. You've had a long, emotional day."

"Thanks, Mom."

"Can I get anyone else a plate while I have the food out?"

"I could go for some food," I tell her, along with Grandpa Jo and Steven.

"I can help you, Mom," Steven offers.

"No need, you just stay seated and I'll have it all ready in just a few minutes."

AN HOUR OR SO LATER, WE'VE ALL EATEN AND HAVE MOVED from the kitchen to the living room. Steven and Renee have packed up Ethan and headed home to get him into bed.

"Did you want to stay here tonight?" Debra asks Lauren.

"I hadn't really thought about where I'd be sleeping tonight. I've been so overwhelmed with everything else going on. Are you and Dad driving home tonight or staying here?"

"I think we'd planned on driving home, and just coming back tomorrow when the rental company is due to be back to break down the tent and pack up all the tables and chairs."

I lean over, wanting to offer up the sanctuary of my hotel room if she'd like to get away from everyone, and say softly, "You're welcome to come to the hotel with me if you need out of here again. It would give us some time alone to talk more."

"Thank you." She gives me a small smile, then turns to her parents. "I might go to the hotel with Sam. I kind of want some time alone to process everything, if you don't mind."

"Whatever you want, we're behind you completely," her dad answers.

"I'm going to head out myself. Call or text me if you need anything," Zoey tells Lauren, pulling her into a hug goodbye before she leaves the room.

"Let me just grab my suitcase from upstairs, and we can

head out," she tells me, then stands and walks out of the room. I turn back to the table and am met with a stern look from Ryan.

"I'm trusting you to take care of my baby girl tonight. She's fragile right now, and I'm trusting you to not let her make any more rash decisions she might regret. I'm not saying she's going to make a decision like that, but don't let her rush into anything serious either. I know enough to know how you feel about her, and Debra filled me in on her reasoning for bolting today. I know she trusts you and feels comfortable with you. So, once again, man to man, I'm asking you to take care of her tonight. I love you like a son, but I won't hesitate to destroy all you hold dear if you mess with my girl."

"You have my word. I'll take care of her tonight, and any other night she'll have me. But I also think she needs time to process what happened today and not rush into anything new. I'm willing to take things slow and follow her lead on whatever is to come between us. If that means we just stay friends, then so be it. But if that means that I get to one day call her my own and give her my last name, then you can be damn sure I'll do that as well."

We shake hands, and he pulls me in for a one-armed man hug, slapping me a little harder than he'd normally do on my back. Steven and I aren't the only ones who go a little alpha-male protective over Lauren. We learned from the best, and he's not afraid to remind me of that fact.

A few moments later, Lauren comes back down the stairs, suitcase in hand, along with a dress bag draped over her free arm.

"Let me just say goodbye to everyone and then I'll be ready to go."

"I'm ready when you are. Are you riding with me?" I ask, not really knowing what her plan is.

"Yes, if you don't mind, I don't have my car here. I'll need to go get it sometime tomorrow."

"Of course, I don't mind. While you say your goodbyes, I'll get your bags loaded up," I tell her, reaching for her things.

I quickly get them into the back seat of my rental, then head back into the house to say goodbye myself and wait for Lauren.

A few minutes later, we're in the car and pulling out on the road.

"Need me to stop anywhere before the hotel?"

"I don't think so. I've got anything I might need tonight in my suitcase, so unless you need something..."

"Nope, I've got everything I need," I tell her, reaching over and grabbing her hand, interlacing our fingers together before I drop them on her leg. My thumb rubs circles on the top of her hand, the softness of her skin making my own skin tingle.

It doesn't take long for us to reach the hotel, and after getting out of the car, I grab Lauren's bags from the back seat. We make our way back up to my room, both quiet as we settle in.

Lauren opens her suitcase, pulling out a toiletries bag and what looks to be some pajamas, or maybe yoga pants and a tank top.

"I'm just going to get ready for bed before we talk, if that's okay with you. I'm exhausted, so I'm not sure how long I'll be able to stay awake tonight."

"Whatever you need. I'm here for you."

I grab my own clothes to change into, figuring it's probably best to sleep in a little more than my boxer briefs, like I normally do. As soon as she closes the door to the bathroom, I strip and pull on a pair of basketball shorts and a t-shirt, then take a seat on the bed to wait for Lauren to join me.

12

LAUREN

I STEP INTO THE BATHROOM, TAKING IN MY APPEARANCE, AND it isn't a lovely sight. I look like I've aged ten years today alone. I guess leaving your fiancé at the altar will do that to a girl.

I quickly change into my sleep tank and shorts, and then pull out my face wash and toothbrush. As I told Sam, I'm exhausted and not sure how long I'm going to last tonight. I think a good night's sleep will do wonders for me.

I quickly finish up in the bathroom and when I exit, I find Sam propped up on the bed, watching some show on the TV. He's also changed into some sleep clothes and, holy shit, does he look good. I have to bite my lip to keep a moan from escaping. *Why did I think staying with him was a good idea?*

"You okay over there?" he asks, pulling me from my daydream ogling fest. Thankfully, he doesn't embarrass me by calling me out on it.

"Oh yeah, sorry. Just lots on my mind," I tell him, trying to pass it off as nothing.

"Come here," he says, patting the bed next to him.

I set my clothes back in my suitcase and make my way over to the king-sized bed. I sit down, then slide over until I'm settled in the center of that side of the bed.

"I'm sorry for all the drama and stress today. Thank you for being here for me," I tell Sam.

"You don't have to apologize to me. I'd rather you follow your heart than do something because you didn't want to upset someone else."

"Thank you." I shift so I'm lying on my side, facing him. I adjust the pillow to help prop me up and get comfortable. "What's your favorite memory from our childhood?" I ask, not really knowing how to jump into the conversation we need to have.

"Hmmm... there are so many good ones. How to choose just one," he muses, then goes silent as he starts thinking. "Do you have one already picked out?"

"I don't necessarily have just one, but many."

"Tell me one."

Lauren

16 years old

THE HOMECOMING FOOTBALL GAME JUST ENDED, AND THE guys played amazing. Not only did they bring home the win, but they kept the other team to only one field goal the entire game. I'm still hanging out in the stands with our group of friends, waiting on the guys to get show- ered and changed before we head for the homecoming party.

"Sam!" I shriek as I'm picked up from behind and swung around in a circle. "Put me down!" I laugh at him as he spins us around a second time before putting me back down on my feet. "What was that for?"

"Just because." He laughs. "I knew you didn't hear me approach and that I'd be able to catch you off guard," he says on another laugh.

"You ready to head out?" I ask, slugging him in the arm.

"Yep," he tells me. I turn and surprise him when I jump on his back for a piggyback ride.

"Let's go!" I giggle in his ear.

He carries me out of the stands and toward the parking lot, as if I weigh nothing. I am holding on to his bag for him so that his arms can be looped around my legs, helping shoulder my weight.

We make it out to his truck and he sets me down on the ground, then grabs his bag from me and tosses it in the bed of the truck.

"You ready for the party tonight?"

"Of course! Wouldn't miss it after the win you guys pulled off."

Lauren
Now

"I'D FORGOTTEN ALL ABOUT THAT NIGHT," SAM TELLS ME, laughing at how animated I got retelling him all about it.

"God, to be in high school again. When our biggest worry was what we were going to do on the weekend, and who was dating who."

"As much fun as we had back then, I wouldn't go back and change it. I truly believe that what we've been through helps pave the way to where we are today. Even the heartache and pain that we've endured is important to our journeys," he tells me.

"I remember we stayed up all night that night, talking and celebrating the win. For whatever reason, it's one of those moments that I always think about. I remember thinking and wishing so much that you'd kiss me that night."

"I remember *wanting* to kiss you that night. It took a lot of self-control to keep my hands and lips off of you," he says.

"I know I'm skipping ahead a few years here, but do you remember shortly after I introduced Brad to you, you started dating Kate?"

"Of course, she was the waitress at the pizza place the night you introduced him to Steven and me. She left her number on the back of my receipt and I was so pissed off that you were dating someone and had kept it from me for so long that I actually texted her. Why?"

"I knew before I started dating Brad that I loved you more than just as my best friend, but you'd never shown me any signs that you were interested in more. So rather than confront you with my feelings, I decided to take control and start dating. I thought that if you felt differently, you'd get pissed off and confront me before my relationship got serious. But then you didn't do anything, and the next time I saw you, you were already dating Kate.

"Then things got serious between Brad and me, so I just kind of gave up hope that anything would ever happen between us. I did my best to focus on my relationship with Brad and not my feelings for you. Looking back, I realize now that the distance between us started then. But it was easy to not notice at the time, as you were busy with football and classes, and I was busy with my own classes and spending time with Brad."

"It was a total dick move, but at first, I only texted Kate to try and make you jealous, and to try and take my mind off of lusting after you. I hid it somehow from Kate for the few months we dated, but she eventually figured things out and dumped my ass. After that, I did a lot of hate fucking the rest of my college years, as I couldn't get over this pull to you. But by then, you'd been dating Brad for so long and I knew it was serious, so I started applying for jobs out of state and the rest is history."

Sam reaches out his hand and pushes the lock of my hair that's slipped from being tucked back out of my face, allowing his fingers to linger against my skin. The heat from his touch has my blood zinging to life. He sinks his hand into my hair and just stares into my eyes.

"I really want to kiss you, but I don't think that's a good idea yet," he whispers.

"I feel the same way," I murmur.

"Come here." He tugs me closer to him as he adjusts how he's sitting on the bed. He lies down, slipping his arm around me, and pulls me so I'm next to him, my head cradled in the crook of his arm. I slip my right arm across his chest, resting my hand over his heart.

We lie there in silence for a little bit. I shift my head to be partly on his chest as he slides his fingers through my hair. The steady thumping of his heartbeat and the soothing feeling of him playing with my hair has me closing my eyes as I fight off falling asleep.

"Tell me another memory," I sleepily tell him.

He is quiet for a few moments, obviously thinking back to our childhood and to a memory that stands out to him.

"Do you remember the first time I got to go camping with your family?"

"Yes! We were, what, eleven or twelve?"

"Twelve, we'd just finished sixth grade." He slips his hand down my side to rest on my hip, giving it a little squeeze.

Sam
12 years old

"ARE YOU KIDS READY TO GO?" MR. KRAMER ASKS THE THREE of us.

"Yep!" Lauren calls out to her dad.

"Then load up, make sure you've gone to the bathroom before we hit the road."

The Kramers are headed out on their annual Memorial Day weekend camping trip and they invited me along this year. I've heard all about this trip, as they make it every year, and I've always wanted to go with them.

Steven heads to the driver's side of the truck, getting in behind his dad's seat, and Lauren and I head for the passenger side, where I open the door up and allow Ren to take the middle seat.

"You kids got all your stuff for the drive?" Mrs. Kramer asks as she climbs in the passenger seat.

"We're all set," Lauren answers her for the three of us.

"Are you excited, Sam?"

"Absolutely, Mrs. Kramer. Thank you again for inviting me to go with you guys this year."

"We're glad you could come along this year. I'm sure you kids will have a great time."

A few hours later, we pull up to the campground. After Mr. Kramer gets the trailer parked in the spot correctly, we all get out and help get everything put together for our stay.

We help unload our bikes and get the camping chairs all set up. Mrs. Kramer sends Steven and me out to collect some more firewood in the woods to use in the fire pit in the evenings. It only takes us about a half hour to collect a good amount of wood to use over the next few days, and if we happen to run out, we can always go out looking for more.

By the time we make it back with the wood, Lauren and her parents had finished up getting the campsite all set up and ready for us to have fun for the next few days.

"You kids ready to head down to the lake, maybe swim for a little while?" Mrs. Kramer asks.

"Yes!" We all cheer.

"Then head in and get changed, and we'll head down to the lake for a few hours."

The three of us take off for the camper and after getting changed, we hop on our bikes and ride down to the lake that's part of the campground.

"Ren, I'll race you to the end of the dock!" I call out to her when we reach the lake.

"You're on!" she volleys back at me.

We both take off running and reach the end of the dock, just about dead even with each other. We both cannonball into the water at the same time, creating a large splash that's made even bigger when Steven cannonballs into the water right after we do.

We all come up sputtering and laughing super hard, splashing each other as we play in the lake. We jump in countless times, swimming out and back from the small dock that's been put up in the lake for swimmers.

Once out of the lake, exhausted and hungry, we head back to our campsite, where Mr. Kramer has started the fire in the fire pit and gotten the grate put on so that we can cook our meal.

"Why don't you kids head inside and get changed before dinner," Mrs. Kramer tells us.

Less than ten minutes later, changed and feeling refreshed, we head back out and sit around the fire.

"Here are some roasting skewers for you to use, and the hot dogs are on a plate over there," Mr. Kramer tells us, handing each of us a skewer as we exit the camper. "I'll get the burgers on the fire shortly, if you'd like one, as well."

"We also have s'mores stuff for after dinner!" Mrs. Kramer tells us excitedly.

We head over to the fire pit, each of us choosing to roast a hot dog for now, as we're all starving after all the time we spent playing in the lake.

As the sun goes down and the stars come out, the excitement of getting to be out here with my two best friends, experiencing this with them after hearing about this trip each year, bubbles up inside of me.

"I was thinking we could go for a bike ride in the morning, if that sounds like a good plan to the three of you," Mrs. Kramer says to us as we relax around the fire.

"Sounds like fun!" I reply to her.

"Then you guys can either find something around the campsite to do, or we can go back down to the lake for the afternoon."

The rest of the weekend went about the same as our first night and was one of the best weekends of my life in my twelve short years. Being an only child, going camping with my parents was nowhere near as fun as it was getting to go with my two best friends.

Sam

Present

"THAT WAS THE FIRST OF MANY FUN CAMPING WEEKENDS! It only got better once my parents finally bought a camper of our own and our families started going together on a more frequent basis."

"It was a fun trip, I'd almost forgotten about it. And it makes me realize how long it's been since I've been out camping. I used to love it so much, but probably haven't been in years."

"We should go sometime this summer! I'm sure we could use one of the campers or could find a place with cabins for rent. Get away and into the woods for a few days together?" I suggest.

"Maybe," she replies on a yawn.

"For now, I think it's time to call it a night and go to sleep."

"Okay." Lauren sighs as her body relaxes even more into me. I just lie there, my eyes closed, but I'm still wide awake. I have Lauren in my arms, curled around my body in a position I never dreamed I would ever get to hold her in, so I'm in no rush to change it or miss any of it.

I'm not sure what's in store for us in the future, and as much as I hope this is just the beginning of us cuddling like this, each and every night, I have to take things slow. She did just walk away from her own damn wedding. It feels like it was such a long time ago, but in reality, it was only hours ago.

I don't know how long I lay there, remembering everything that happened today; soaking in Lauren and this moment. I eventually drift off to sleep, content, at least for now, simply to have this woman in my arms.

13

LAUREN

I WAKE UP SUDDENLY, FORGETTING FOR A FEW MOMENTS where exactly I am. I have a warm body plastered against my back with an arm wrapped around my torso and a hand cupping my breast. A very pronounced erection is pressed against my back and I wiggle against it. After a groan falls from the lips of the man who I'm wrapped up in, I remember exactly where I am and that I'm not in a bed with my fiancé...err, *ex*-fiancé...I'm in a bed with Sam.

As I lie here, internally freaking the fuck out, all the memories from yesterday come flooding back. The weight of it all comes crushing down on me again and tears fill my eyes, but I'm able to blink them back and keep them from falling.

I finally squirm my way out of Sam's grasp without waking him, and slip from the bed into the bathroom. After shutting the door, I flip on the light and I take one look in the mirror, shuddering at my appearance. My hair looks like a freaking rats' nest, and I'm sure it's not going to be pretty when I go to brush it out later. After going to the bathroom and washing my hands, I quickly brush my teeth and splash some cold water onto my face. As I'm finishing up, I hear a knock on the door and Sam's gravelly voice on the other side.

"Everything okay, Ren?"

"Yes," I tell him as I open the door. I take in his sleep rumpled look, a sliver of his obliques peeking out the side of his t-shirt, where it's ridden up on the side. "Just going to the bathroom and brushing my teeth."

"Did you sleep okay?"

"Yes, better than I expected."

"Good," he says, as I step out of the bathroom and brush past him. He slips an arm around my waist, pulling me against him and wrapping me in a hug.

"What did you want to do today?" he finally asks.

I let out a deep breath, taking a moment to think about everything I need to do today, and how my plans have drastically changed.

I was supposed to be leaving on a flight for my honeymoon.

I was supposed to be experiencing the best days of my life so far.

I was supposed to be sitting on a beach with the love of my life wrapped around me, as we watched the sun set over the water.

But I can't dwell on what today was supposed to be. I have to pull up my big girl panties and move on with my life. I made the decision yesterday to walk away from Brad, and now I have to live with that choice. I don't regret the decision, but I do regret letting it get to the point that it did. I should have told him sooner. I should have called it off before he was standing at the end of the aisle, waiting on me to walk to him.

I'm sure he'll think I'm a bitch, and I'll own that. But I

really do believe that I did us both a favor by not allowing the wedding to go on.

"I should head back over to the farm and help with the teardown of everything. I'm going to figure out how to pay my parents back for everything."

"Do you know what time the rental company is coming by to pick everything up?"

"I think around ten. I'd have to text my mom to verify. I wasn't supposed to be here today, so I'm not exactly sure. After they pick everything up, I'm not sure what to do. I'm kinda still in a fog with everything."

"Okay, well, how about this. You go take a shower and get ready. While you're doing that, I'll pick us up some coffee and breakfast. Then, I can take a quick shower and we'll head to your grandparents' house to help with the teardown. Once we're done with that, let's get away for a few days. We can drive to anywhere, hell, grab a last-minute flight and go somewhere fun or warm, and just get away. I think you could use a few days to decompress."

I groan at the thought of getting away for a few days. It sounds like the perfect thing to do, and what the hell, all my other plans have changed for the week. I already have the time off, so I might as well enjoy it.

"Yes. Yes, to all of it," I tell Sam before I can chicken out.

"Really?" he asks, the surprise filling his voice.

"Yes. I just need to get away for a few days. I told Brad that I would stop at our place to box my things up, so maybe we can do that this afternoon and leave tomorrow? I'll text him first to make sure today is okay with him. Where should we go?"

"You pick. This getaway is all for you to relax and unwind. If you want to do that on a beach, then we'll go to the beach. If you want to do that at a cabin in the woods, then we'll head to the Smoky Mountains. You want to hit up New York City or Vegas, then we'll make that happen," Sam says, placing a kiss to my forehead.

The feel of his lips against me has my skin prickling and the blood pumping in my body. I know we need to take things slow, and I know Sam would never push me to do anything I didn't feel okay with. I think that's why I was so comfortable coming here with him last night. Why I feel comfortable enough to get away with him for a few days.

"Okay, let's get moving. I'll head out to grab us that coffee and breakfast, and you work on getting yourself ready to face the day."

Before I let Sam go, I look up at him, our eyes connecting, and a silent conversation flows between the two of us.

I love you, I'll wait for you. You're it for me, his eyes tell me, while mine say, *I love you. I always have, and I always will. Please be patient with me. Please stay by my side. I promise, one day, I'll be yours forever, and you'll be mine.*

"Thank you for everything. I don't know what I'd do without you the last fifteen or so hours. Just promise me that you'll be patient with me. I'm going to need time to figure out my life, and with that will come some decisions for the two of us to make together. I just can't guarantee when that time will come. I don't know if I'll be ready to have those discussions in a few weeks, months, or maybe even a year. I think I'm going to need some time to just be me, figure out the new me."

"I'll be here when you're ready." He drops his forehead to mine. "I've waited for you for this long, I can wait a little more."

"Okay, let's get moving. I'll send Brad a quick text before I jump in the shower to make sure he's okay with today."

We both step back from the embrace we've been in for

the past few minutes. I grab my phone and shoot off a text as Sam slips on his flip flops and grabs his wallet and keys from the table, then heads out the door.

Lauren: Hey, sorry to bother you so early, but I was hoping to go to the condo this afternoon and start packing my stuff. I just wanted to give you a heads up.

I toss my phone on the bed, then stop at my overnight bag and grab some clean clothes to take into the bathroom with me.

I let the hot water wash over my skin, the heat from the water seeping into my body as it warms me up. I finally reach for the shampoo and get on with my shower, so I can possibly be dressed once Sam returns with our coffee and breakfast.

Just as I come out of the bathroom, Sam is walking back through the door, hands filled with a drink carrier and a bag full of greasy goodness for breakfast. I quickly reach out, grabbing the drinks from him.

"The one with the sticker over the opening is yours," he tells me.

"Thank you, I owe you." I quickly remove the sticker covering the opening on my cup and lift it to my lips. The aroma hits my nose and I inhale the coffee smell. I can instantly feel the calmness soaking into my body. I take a tentative sip, not wanting to burn my mouth, and once I know it isn't going to scald me, I take a heftier drink. I can feel the jolt of adrenaline as the caffeine hits my system.

"Did you hear back from Brad?" Sam asks as he sets the bag filled with the food on the small table.

"Oh, let me check. I left my phone out here on the bed." I grab my phone and see a text from Brad waiting for me.

Brad: Yeah, sure whenever you want. I just didn't think it would be so quick. Can we talk when you come over?

Lauren: I think it would be better to talk in a few days. I think I'm going to get out of town for a few days just to decompress, but once I'm back we can meet for lunch or something if you'd like.

Brad: Yeah, sure Lauren, whatever works for you. I'll stay away from the condo this afternoon so that you can get your things. Just let me know when you're back in town and we can get together.

Lauren: Thank you, and I'll let you know.

I toss my phone back on the bed and walk over to the small table, dropping down in one of the chairs.

"Everything okay?"

"Yeah, Brad just asked if we can talk again. I'm going to let him know once we're back, and we'll get together. He'd originally wanted to talk when I came over later today, but I told him I thought it would be best to talk when I get back and he agreed to that."

I pick up the breakfast sandwich Sam has placed in front of me and take a huge bite of it, moaning just as my stomach rumbles super loud. Loud enough that both Sam and I burst out laughing.

We finish up our breakfast, and Sam disappears into the bathroom to take his shower. I've got a lot to get done in the next day or so, and need to get a start on it if I'm going to be able to enjoy myself when we're gone.

14

LAUREN

WE PULL UP TO MY GRANDPARENTS' HOUSE AND THE RENTAL company is already here. They've already broken down the tent and have all the chairs on the racks. Realizing they have everything under control, we head inside to find my parents and grandparents sitting around the table drinking coffee.

"Morning, sweetheart," my dad calls out. "How are you holding up?"

"I'm good. How are things going here?"

"Just fine, the rental company has everything under control, and should be out of here within the next half hour or so. Got any plans today?"

"Yeah, here in a little while, we're going to head over to the condo so I can start packing up my stuff. When I talked with Brad yesterday, I told him I'd let him keep the condo. So, is it okay with you guys if I store my things in the garage and stay in my old room until I can find a new apartment to move into?"

"Of course you can," my mom pipes up. "You know your room is still there for you whenever you need it, and for however long you need it."

"Thanks. I promise I won't move back for long. I'll start looking for an apartment in the next week or so."

"Don't feel like you have to rush. If you want to stay a couple months to save up some money, you're more than welcome to do that as well."

"Well, thank you for the offer. We can talk more about it later. Sam and I are going to get out of town for a few days. I think we're going to try and leave tomorrow."

"Oh," my mom says, the surprise evident in her voice. "Where are you guys going to go?"

"We're not sure yet," Sam answers her. "I told Ren to pick a place, and we'll either drive or see if we can find a last-minute flight. Figured she could do with getting away for a few days to just relax, and I have until next week off."

"Well, that was nice of you. I'm sure you guys will have a good time, no matter where you go," my mom says.

My phone pings with a new text, drawing my attention to it.

Zoey: Hey girlie. How are you holding up today? Did you get any sleep last night?

Lauren: As good as I can be. I actually slept really well last night. I think it helped being away from the house. Sam was so kind and comforting to me last night.

Zoey: That's good to hear. What're your plans for today and this week?

Lauren: I'm actually headed over to the condo soon to pack up some of my stuff and move it over to my parents' house. Sam asked if I wanted to get away for a few days, so we're going to pick a place and get out of town. I think we'll pick somewhere on the beach.

Zoey: Keep me posted. I love that you're following your

heart and going after what you truly want. No need to settle in life, girl.

Zoey: I want to hear how things went with Brad and how packing up the condo goes. If you need help with that, I'm just a call or text away.

Lauren: Once I'm back, we can plan a girls' night and drink copious amounts of wine and I'll tell you everything. Promise.

WE FINALLY LEAVE MY GRANDPARENTS' HOUSE, AND HEAD FOR the condo Brad and I have shared for the past year. My grandparents sent us with a collection of boxes they had in the garage, so I could have something to pack all my things into.

We walk into the condo, finding it dark. It doesn't look like Brad has even been here yet, which is always possible. I take a look around, really looking at this place I've called home for the past year.

"How about I get some of these boxes made up for you, and you can decide where you want to start."

"Thanks. I'll go pull out my empty suitcases and duffel bags to start with my clothes. I can always come back another day to work on my other things. I don't think I'm going to take much of the furniture or kitchen stuff. I'll just buy all new stuff when I get my own place. I don't feel like 'fighting over the silverware', ya know."

"Whatever you want to do."

I head to the bedroom and pull out the two suitcases that are stored under the bed. I open them up on the bed and head for my closet. I start pulling out my summer things first, as I'm going to need all of that. The winter stuff and my work clothes can all go in boxes; I won't need it all until fall, when school is back in session and I'm back in my classroom.

"Here's a couple of the boxes, can I help with anything?" Sam asks, walking into the room.

"Sure, I figured I could put my winter and work clothes in the boxes as I won't need any of them for now, so if you want to start grabbing them and filling the boxes, that would be great."

We both work on emptying out my closet, and I move onto the bathroom to get my things. By the time I have all of my things from there, the suitcase and boxes we started are full.

"Do you want me to make up any more of the boxes?" Sam asks, as we tape shut the last full box.

"I don't know. I can always come back in a few days and finish packing my stuff, if you want to get out of here."

"I'm here to help, so if you want to keep going, then we'll keep going. If you want to get out of here, then we'll load up these things and hit the road."

"Is all of this going to even fit in the car?"

"Yep, it should. We probably can't fit much more, but the boxes will fit in the back seat, and the suitcases in the trunk. We could probably fit another box in the back, and some smaller ones in the trunk."

"I think I'm ready to be done for today. Let me just look around and make sure I don't see anything that I'll need in the next few days and then we can get out of here. We can leave the unused boxes here, so that I have them when I do come back to finish packing up."

"Sounds good. While you check around, I'll start loading

everything. Once we leave, we can go drop it all off at your parents' house, and then maybe grab some takeout somewhere and take it back to the hotel. We can pull out my laptop and figure out where we want to get away to."

"That sounds like the perfect plan," I tell him, pushing up on my toes to kiss his cheek.

Sam grabs one of the boxes and I open the door for him, then start my sweep of each room. I find a few more items that I place in an empty basket to carry down with me to the car.

I'm in the living room when I hear the door open, figuring it's Sam grabbing another box. I don't pay much attention to it, so I'm caught off guard when I turn around and find Brad standing in the doorway.

"Oh shit!" I shout as I jump slightly. "You scared the hell out of me."

"Sorry, didn't mean to. Did you need any help?"

My heart aches at Brad's appearance. He looks like utter shit, not that I probably look any better. But I can tell he hasn't slept much, and it looks like he's cried some.

Fuck, there's that feeling again.

I know I hurt him, I know what I did was a bitch move, but I had to follow my heart.

"I was just doing a quick sweep to make sure there wasn't anything I couldn't do without for the next few days. I only packed up my clothes and bathroom things for now. I'll come back in a few days to pack up everything else. I have some boxes, so if you come across anything that's mine and you want it out of your way, feel free to put it into a box. It might be next weekend or early next week before I'm back."

His eyes are downcast, staring at the floor as I tell him my plans.

78

"Okay," he says on a long breath. "And we'll still talk then?" A little thread of hope laces his voice.

"Yes, of course," I tell him, as I hear the door open again and this time, I know it's Sam coming back in.

"Hey, you about ready?" Sam asks, coming to a stop when he notices Brad in the room.

"Just about. Are you still loading everything?"

"Just one more load, unless you have anything else."

"Just a few things, but I can get them. Can you just give me another minute, please?"

"Sure, I'll wait for you down in the car."

"Thank you. I'll be down in just a few minutes."

Sam turns to leave, and I can feel the tension in the room. By the look on Brad's face, I'm guessing he thinks I've already moved on to Sam. He probably thinks I fucked him last night.

The silence between us lingers until it's uncomfortable.

"I'm going to go. I'll text you when I'm back in town and we can get together," I say, my voice barely a whisper.

"Lauren, please don't go," he replies. "Please, baby. I love you." He takes a step closer to me, cupping my cheek with one hand, and places the other on my opposite hip. "We can work through all of this and make it work. I don't know what I'd do without you."

Tears fill my eyes as his words hit me, each one like a bullet straight to my heart. I knew, by leaving him, I'd be breaking his heart, but I can't stay with him just because he loves me. It isn't that I don't love Brad, because I do. It's just that my love for Sam is so much stronger.

"I'm sorry. I just can't," I tell him, as the tears spill from my eyes and down my cheeks. He swipes at the ones his thumb can reach, helping to wipe them away.

We both look at each other as my words settle between

the two of us. I can see the effect they have on him, hitting him almost as his words pierced me. He drops his hand from my face and takes a small step back. The look of rejection rolls off of him and fractures my heart again as I take on the guilt that I did this to him, I caused this hurt.

"I'm sorry. I'm going to go now. I'll talk to you later." I grab the basket and leave the condo. Just before I close the door, I can hear him lose his control and break down. It hits me hard and takes all my strength to not collapse there outside the door. I make it down to the car, the tears still streaming down my face.

Sam jumps out and wraps me in his arms before I can get the door open.

"Shhh, shhh." He tries to calm me down, grabbing the basket from my arms and setting it on the top of the car, before wrapping an arm around my shoulders and one hand holding my head tightly against him, offering me his comfort. "Everything's going to be fine."

"He asked me to stay, told me he still loved me, and we could work it all out," I finally get out between the tears.

"I'm sorry. I wish I could take all your pain away, Ren," Sam says, placing a kiss against my temple as he continues to hold me tight. The emotional toll I've been through the past twenty-four hours is hitting me hard again, and I feel like I could collapse and sleep for a week.

I pull myself together enough to stop the tears so that Sam will let me go. We both climb into the car and he pulls out onto the road.

Lauren: Packing up went well until Brad showed up. Tried to get me to stay. Told me we could work through whatever this was and that he still loved me and always would. Zoey, please tell me I did the right thing.

Zoey: Oh, Ren. If leaving Brad was what your heart was telling you to do, then it was absolutely the right thing to do. Don't let him make you feel any differently. Give him some time and he'll eventually realize that you didn't leave him to be mean, you were just following your heart.

15

SAM

After dropping the carload of things off at Lauren's parents' house, we stop in to say a quick hello to my parents. My mom insists on feeding us, so after dinner, we finally get out of there and are just getting back to the hotel.

"I'm exhausted and so full," Ren tells me as we walk down the hotel hallway. This entire situation with Lauren leaving Brad has me glad I decided to get a hotel this trip rather than stay at my parents' house in my old room. Sleeping on the old twin bed from my childhood doesn't sound appealing to me anymore, so a hotel is worth every penny I'm paying.

"How does a hot, relaxing bath sound? Take advantage of the jetted tub in the bathroom," I suggest.

"That sounds heavenly."

I pull out the key card and tap it against the door, then let Lauren walk in the room before me.

"I'll start filling the tub for you, so grab your stuff," I say, stepping into the oversized bathroom and turning on the water. It takes it a few minutes to get hot, but once it does, I drop the stopper. Rummaging through the items the hotel has on the counter, I find some bath salts that I sprinkle in the water.

I pull down one of the towels and place it on the edge of the tub, so that Lauren has it within reach when she's ready to get out, as well as one of the bathrobes that were hanging on the back of the door.

"All ready for you in here," I call out to her.

She walks in, clean pajamas in her hand. The events of the last day is evident on her face, but even with all the stress and crying she's been through, she's still the most beautiful woman to me.

"I'll get out of your way. Holler if you need anything."

"Thanks, Sam," she tells me, placing her hand on my arm and giving it a quick squeeze before I walk out of the bathroom, pulling the door closed behind me.

I drop onto one of the chairs surrounding the small table and blow out a big breath. I would have never in a million years guessed that the past twenty-four would have gone the way it has.

I tap the enter button on my laptop, waking it up so I can start searching for a place for us to get away to for the next few days.

"Hey, Ren. I'm going to run downstairs and grab a beer from the bar, do you want anything? Wine? Cocktail?" I call through the door.

"Um, sure. Either a glass of wine or a Malibu Pineapple would be great."

"Okay, I'll be right back." I grab my wallet and key card off the table.

The bar is a little busy, so it takes me twenty or so minutes to get our drinks. As I open the room door, Lauren is coming out of the bathroom, all wrapped up in the bathrobe, with her hair wrapped in a towel on the top of her head. She looks completely relaxed and her natural beauty knocks the breath from my lungs.

"Thank you," she's saying to me, when I realize she'd been talking to me. She reaches for the glass in my left hand, taking the drink I brought back for her.

I take a swig of my beer to help give me a second to clear my head. The lust is overtaking my senses tonight.

"You're welcome. I wasn't sure what kind of wine you were in the mood for, so I just went with the Malibu Pineapple."

"It's perfect," she says, taking another sip of the drink.

"I was thinking we could look at places to try and get away to tomorrow. Had you thought of any ideas yet?"

"I'm thinking the beach somewhere. Think we could find any last minute four-day cruises?"

"Maybe, let's sit down and we can check." I motion to the table. We both take a seat around my computer, and I start pulling up different travel sites. Lauren also pulls out her iPad, so she can look up options, as well.

After pouring over a few options, we finally decided on renting an Airbnb down in Destin, Florida for four nights. We'll drive all day tomorrow, so that we don't have to rent a car, and then drive back next weekend. This works out perfectly, as we'll only be across the street from the beach.

———

WE HIT THE ROAD EARLY THIS MORNING, AROUND SIX. I offered to start the drive so that Lauren could get some more sleep. She fell asleep for the first few hours, and I just enjoyed the drive with her in the car with me; I didn't care that she was sound asleep. Just having her close to me was enough to make me happy for now.

I pull off the interstate for a bathroom break and coffee refill, and the slowing of the car wakes her up. She lifts her arms to stretch and her shirt rides up on her side, allowing me a peek of her skin. What I wouldn't do to rub my fingers and then tongue against that skin. The idea has my dick hardening in my jeans and pushing against my zipper. I adjust myself as discreetly as I can, sitting here next to her.

"Have a good nap?" I ask, finally breaking the silence between us.

"Yes, thank you for letting me get some more sleep. I promise I'll be a better road trip buddy from here on out."

We both get out of the car and make our way into the store. I head first for the bathroom and then grab a large cup of coffee and look over their breakfast selections. After settling on a breakfast sandwich, I meet up with Lauren at the counter and pay for our few items.

"You don't have to pay for everything for me, you know," she tells me, bumping her shoulder into mine as we walk out to the car.

"I know, but I want to," I tell her honestly.

"Please let me pay for the groceries or something once we make it down. I'll feel like too much of a leach if you pay for this entire trip. It isn't fair to you to pay for everything."

"We'll see," I tell her, a smirk on my face.

"Did you want me to drive for a while?" she asks as we reach the car.

"I'm still good if you want to keep riding shotgun."

"Sure, I'll play DJ and keep the music pumping." She laughs.

The melody of her laugh washes over me as we both get settled into the car and back out on the road.

Lauren finds us a country station to listen to for a while, bouncing a bit in her seat.

"I see you found the coffee." I laugh at her excitement, teasing her just a bit.

"Nah, I'm just excited to be headed to the beach. Thank you for thinking of getting away with me. I really appreciate it."

"Anytime, Ren, anytime," I tell her, reaching over to squeeze her knee. I leave my hand on her leg and notice she doesn't make any attempt to remove it. If anything, she settles in a little closer and gets comfortable with my skin against her skin.

The miles pass as we both sing along with the songs on the radio. When "Marry Me" by Thomas Rhett comes on the radio, she leans over and turns up the volume, and starts belting the words out along with the song. I just sit back and listen to the lyrics, and it hits me how much this song reminds me of the two of us.

The song ends, and she turns the volume back down to a normal level.

"So, we've got lots of time ahead of us on the road. Tell me about life in North Carolina."

"What do you want to know?"

"Everything. I feel like I don't know anything about you from the last couple of years. Steven only mentioned you occasionally."

"Not much to know, really. I moved out there for my job right after graduation. I like my job and it pays me well, so I've stayed. I've made some good friends in the area, but it still doesn't feel like home. Not the way Kentucky does."

"Have you thought of moving back?"

"The thought has crossed my mind a time or two. I just didn't think I could be back around here, with you marrying Brad."

"Is that a possibility now?"

"Hopefully. I keep an eye on the open positions at the local office. That's the nice thing about working for the FBI. I can pretty much move anywhere within the USA, and a position would be available to me."

"You don't ever have to go out in the field, do you?"

"No, I'm not a field agent. I stay in my office, for the most part, sometimes move to a large situation debriefing room, if we're working on a large case and there is a lot of information to give the field agents. That's the beauty of being on the IT side of things. I stay put and am safe. I only carry a gun because it's a requirement of all agents."

"Do you enjoy your job?"

"Most days. I like tracking down the bad guys, just like most agents do. I just prefer to be behind the screen of my computer when I do it. With all the cyber crimes taking place these days, my department stays busy all of the time."

"Have you worked on any high-profile cases?"

"A few. None that probably made the news here, but locally, they were very big deals."

"I'm glad to know you're safe. I'd worry about you being out in the field, dealing with the big-time criminal."

I chuckle at that. "How's teaching going?"

"It's everything I dreamed of and more. I love all my students. I never thought I'd enjoy teaching third grade, but it is quickly becoming one of my favorite grades to teach."

"Do you think you'll stay at the same school?"

"That's my hope. The staff is all amazing. We have a great administration, and everyone gets along well. That's not always the case in some schools. I have friends at other schools and the drama amongst the teachers is pretty bad. Makes me thankful for where I'm at."

"Do you think they'll keep you teaching third grade?"

"I hope so. But depending on the student numbers each

year, we sometimes have to change up how many classes they have per grade level, to keep the class sizes at a more reasonable number. This last school year, I had twenty-one students. The registration numbers for next year are predicting third grade to have classes with twenty-three or twenty-four kids. My principal doesn't like to have more than twenty-five per class if she can swing it, so hopefully we'll stay under that number, or have enough overage that they'd move teachers around to accommodate the influx."

"Do you get to take your students on any fun field trips?"

"I do! In the fall, we go out to the nature reserve for a day, and in the winter, we usually go to a performance at the Performing Arts Center downtown. They put on a special production of whatever show they are running for the schools at a discounted price. And then, in the spring, we usually go to the zoo for the day. Different grade levels do different things, but the PTA helps fund the trips, paying for the buses for all the classes to take three field trips a year, as well as helping with scholarships for any kids whose parents might not be able to afford the cost of the trip for their kids."

"Do you have to supply a lot of your own supplies? I've heard that many teachers spend a good amount of their own money to keep their classrooms running."

"Yes. The districts' budgets are so tight lately that teachers end up spending a lot of our own money on supplies. Once again, I'm luckier than some of my friends who are at other schools and don't have as supportive of a PTA, or the parents in general. The school I'm at is in a pretty mid to upper-level income area, so the parents are usually great about donating supplies to the classroom when I send out a wish list to them. But when all the school supplies come out and are on sale, I go in and stock up on the basics, so that I at least have them on hand and am getting them at a discount. You'd be shocked how many pencils a classroom of third graders can go through in a day!" she tells me on a laugh.

We continue our conversation over the next few hours of driving, discussing everything from music to politics. The easiness between us is slowly returning, that we'd unfortunately lost over the last couple of years, due to the distance. We stopped a few more times; once for lunch and then a couple other times to stretch our legs and a quick bathroom break.

We made it to Destin just before dinnertime, and after checking into the small condo we rented, we headed out to find some dinner and explore the area just a bit.

16

LAUREN

I WAKE UP FROM THE SUN SHINING IN THE WINDOW AND LOOK out at the beautiful view of the ocean. While we're not directly on the beach, we're just across the street, and since the condo we rented is a few floors up, we have a beautiful view of the water. I roll onto my side, just admiring our surroundings. I could totally move somewhere like this and wake up to this view everyday.

Lauren: Just wanted to let you know we made it down to Destin. Our condo is perfect! It has amazing views and I can already tell this was the perfect place to come to for the next few days.
Zoey: Enjoy! I wish I'd been able to come with you! Don't do anything I wouldn't do! 😜 xoxo

I hear movement out in the kitchen, and a few moments later, can smell the coffee brewing. I finally stretch one last time and drag myself out of bed. After a quick pit stop in the bathroom to pee and brush my teeth, I make my way out to the kitchen, where I find Sam. He's leaning against the counter, looking out the large kitchen window, athletic shorts hanging low off his hips, and looking sleepy and sexy as ever, as he drinks his coffee. The sight of his rippled back and tight ass has my heart jumping a little as I take him all in, and it sends some tingles down my body, right to my core.

God, give me strength.

"Good morning," I finally get out, causing him to turn in my direction.

"Morning, did you sleep well?" he asks, a lazy smile on his face.

"I did. That bed was very comfortable. How about you?"

"Slept great. Did you want some breakfast?"

"Yes, but don't we need to go to the store first? We never made it to one last night."

"There are a few things in the fridge, eggs being one that the note says we can use. I figured we could hit up the store once we've gotten ready. Or, we can get ready and go grab some breakfast somewhere down the beach, then hit up the store. Either is fine with me," he tells me as I grab a cup of coffee for myself.

"I don't need anything big, I'd be fine just grabbing a pastry at the store."

"Let's make up a list, and we can get ready and head out then." He sets his coffee cup down on the counter, and pulls up his notes app on his phone.

A few hours later, we've eaten, the condo kitchen is stocked, and we've packed ourselves a little cooler to take to the beach, where we're headed to now.

"I think I see a good place just down this way where we

can set up," Sam tells me as we approach the sand. I follow him as we make our way just down the beach where there's an opening. Thankfully, the condo we rented provided beach chairs, a canopy thing for shade, and beach towels, as well as a little wagon to bring it all to and from with us.

We both get to work setting up the canopy and chairs, then relax on the beach chairs once we've settled everything.

I lie back in the chair, soaking in the sun, allowing myself to just relax and let go of everything. It feels good to simply kick back and not worry.

"Want something to drink?" Sam asks, opening the cooler we brought.

"Sure, I'll take one of the daiquiris." While at the store, we picked up some already frozen pre-made drinks that you just have to open. Best invention ever.

Sam tears the top off and dumps the slushy mix into a tumbler, then hands it over to me. He pops the top on a beer, placing it in a beer koozie he grabbed at the store.

"Dang, that's tasty," I tell him, after taking my first sip of the drink. "I wasn't sure if it would taste very good being pre-mixed."

"Did you want to do anything else today?" Sam asks as he looks around at what all is going on down the beach.

"I'm happy to just keep my butt planted here on the beach for most of the day. But if there was something you wanted to do, we can do it."

"Nothing specific. Just wanted to make sure with you. Maybe tomorrow, we can get out and explore the area."

"That sounds perfect. I wouldn't mind going up and looking around the touristy area. All those shops looked fun, and the food trucks looked pretty amazing," I say.

"We can definitely head back down and explore the

area. Did you want to go check out the trucks for dinner tonight, or did you want to cook back at the condo?"

"I'm fine with either. We might not feel like cooking after being here at the beach all afternoon, so let's play it by ear."

"Sounds good to me," Sam says, taking another drink from his beer.

We both kick back and soak in the sun some more. I pull out my kindle, pulling up my latest romance novel that's been filling up my long neglected to-be-read list. As I get lost in the story, I forget where I am until I hear Sam laughing next to me.

"What?" I ask him, dropping my kindle onto my chest.

"You must have been reading something really good over there. You were practically squirming in your seat, and you might have moaned a time or two."

"Shut up, no I didn't!"

"Um, yes you did! What were you reading? Something sexy?"

The way his voice dropped when he said *sexy* has my insides waking up even more than they already are after the sex scene I just finished reading.

"Maybe. It's just a romance book."

"A dirty romance book?" he asks, eyebrows bouncing up and down.

"Not dirty, just steamy in a few spots." I finish off my drink and try to cool myself off from not only the heat of the sun, but also from the blush that's kicked up my body heat a few degrees from the embarrassment.

"I knew it!" He practically cheers. "I knew you were reading something that made you all hot and bothered. Don't worry, I won't tell anyone about it," he teases.

"Don't be an ass!" I whisper-yell at him, as I lean over and smack him in the chest. *Wrong move, Lauren.* His chest is a nice hard wall of muscle, and it's currently bare and sweaty. The short few seconds of contact my hand makes with it sends tingles up my body, and I just want to run my hands all over his skin.

He cracks up at me, and it feels so good to be laughing with him. Sam was—*is*—one of my best friends, and has been for most of my life. I didn't realize just how much I missed him being in my life until the past couple of days. I knew I did, but when my focus was always on something else and he wasn't around, we just grew apart. It also doesn't help that we were both harboring hidden feelings for each other.

"Want to go for a walk along the water?" he asks, once we both stop laughing.

"Sure," I answer, tucking my kindle back in my bag.

We walk down the beach, taking in the beauty of the view. The beach is pretty popular, so we dodge kids playing in the sand with their parents, and some college-aged kids playing a game of beach volleyball as we walk along the water's edge.

We make it to a stretch where not many people are crowded in, and the sun has started to drop some, so the sky is turning some beautiful colors. Sam slides his arm around my shoulders, pulling me even closer to his side as we walk in a comfortable silence.

"It's so pretty," I finally say, my eyes still on the setting sun.

"I agree," he replies, and I can feel his eyes on me.

We slow down as we reach the end of the public beach area, standing there against the boardwalk, and just watch the sun sink lower as the water laps at our feet.

"Should we head back and pack everything up, and go find some dinner? I'm getting kind of hungry."

"Sounds like a plan. The food trucks still sound like a good plan to you for tonight?" he asks.

"Yes, I'm in no mood to cook tonight, so the food trucks sound perfect."

We start our walk back to where our stuff is set up. We'd walked a pretty good distance down the beach, so it takes us a little bit to make it back to the spot. With the sun setting fairly quickly, the beach has started to clear out as the families all pack up for the day. As we walk along the water's edge, Sam drops his arm from my shoulders and slips his hand into mine, linking our fingers together.

We walk hand in hand the rest of the way. We both know that I'm not ready to jump into another relationship quite yet. I need time to find myself again, let the dust settle from my relationship with Brad. We were together for a long time, and no matter how I feel about Sam, that doesn't change how big a part of my life Brad was.

Even with all that, it still feels nice to be here with Sam. The small touches make me feel alive and ready to explore what can be between the two of us when the time is right. I just don't know yet how long that will be.

We make it back to our spot, and Sam gets to taking down the shade tent as I collapse the chairs. We get everything loaded back in the wagon and make the walk across the street and back to the condo.

"I think I'm going to take a quick shower to rinse off all the sand and sunscreen before we leave for dinner, if that's okay with you?" I ask him as we enter the condo.

"I was thinking of doing the same thing. Meet you back out here in thirty minutes or so?"

"Perfect." I walk into my room, shutting the door behind me, then slip out of my swim coverup and bikini.

17

SAM

After a quick shower, I dress in some khaki shorts and a polo shirt, then head out to the living room to wait on Lauren.

I pull out my phone, checking my missed texts from this afternoon. I have one from my mom and a couple from Steven, both checking in to make sure we made it down here to the beach all right, and making sure Lauren is holding up okay. I shoot back texts to both of them, letting everyone know we made it and that we're doing fine.

Once I've got the texts replied to, I pull up my work email and make sure I haven't been sent anything that can't wait until I return next week. I'd wrapped up the large case I'd been working on before I left, so I'm not surprised when nothing is waiting on me.

A few minutes later, Lauren comes out and the sight of her has the air rushing out of my lungs. She's dressed in a simple sun dress that hugs her curves. It shows off the swell of her breasts, the dip of her waist, and the flare of her hips. It takes all of my self control to not jump from the couch and gather her up in my arms, marching us back to one of the beds where I'd strip us both of our clothes and sink so far inside her that we wouldn't know where I ended, and she began.

I adjust myself as discreetly as possible, my dick now hard as a steel rod and pushing against the zipper of my shorts.

"Ready?" I finally get out as I stand from the couch.

"Yes, and I'm starving, so let's get food first before we walk around."

"After you," I tell her, lifting my arm to usher her out of the condo.

We walk the half or so mile down to the center of the town, where all the shops and food trucks are located. After a quick loop around to see what our food options are, we decide on the seafood truck advertising local specialties that are freshly caught daily. We settle on a large order of the steamed shrimp, enough for us to share. We make our way to the tables and find a spot to eat as the sound of the musicians up on the small stage fills the air.

"Oh my God, these are amazing," Lauren moans as she takes a bite.

"I agree. I don't think I've ever had such fresh shrimp."

"I could eat this everyday we're here and I'd be happy," she says between bites.

We don't get much talking in as we both devour our food. She wasn't wrong when she said this meal was amazing.

We finish eating and listen to the music playing. The band up on the stage is doing a great job entertaining the crowd, getting people up and dancing and having a good time. They sing a wide range of popular songs, from country to top-40 hits, a little bit of rock and roll, and even an R&B song thrown in.

"I'm going to go check out some of the little shops, did you want to come with me?" Lauren asks, after we've listened to the band play for a while.

"Sure, let's go," I say, standing and picking up the tray full of trash. After I toss it all in the bin and place the tray in the cart, we walk toward the strip of shops lining the court-yard area we'd been sitting in.

I reach out and twine my fingers with Lauren's as we walk along the sidewalk. I love the feeling of her skin against mine, and she hasn't seemed to mind the few other times I've held her hand. I know I need to give her time and space, and I will. But this is one small way we can feel connected in the meantime. She turns her head to me, giving me a small coy smile once our fingers are interlocked together.

"Oh, I want to go inside this place!" Lauren excitedly tells me, pulling me slightly into the shop.

We are greeted by the sales clerk as soon as we step inside. We browse the traditional touristy items—t-shirts, sweatshirts, shot glasses, post cards, and so much more. We separate as we each browse the items, and I'm looking through some of the funny trinkets they have when Lauren comes up with a few items in her hands.

"Find some good things?"

"Yeah, just a couple tank tops and a floatie to take out in the water when we go back to the beach."

We make our way to the checkout and Lauren quickly pays for her items. I take the bag from her as we exit the store, and immediately slide my hand back into hers as we walk along the sidewalk.

"Want to grab some ice cream?" I ask, as we approach a store advertising freshly-made ice cream and other desserts.

"Sure, I could go for a cone," she says, smiling up at me

before she lifts up on her toes and kisses my cheek. Damn, what I would do to turn my head slightly and capture her lips with my own. But due time, and all that jazz. I know we'll have that moment, now just isn't the time for it. When the time is right and we're ready to take that next step, I'll damn well make that first real kiss between the two of us something neither one of us will ever forget.

We each have a hard time selecting what flavors we want as so many of them sound so good. We each end up with a double scoop cone and take them back outside to eat while we stroll along, checking out the shops some more. We each selected two different flavors and share them with each other as we walk along. Once we reach the end of the shops, we head in the direction of the condo.

The area we're in is very pedestrian-friendly, as most people are going and coming from the beach all day. A few bars can now be seen, with areas down on the beach roped off, hanging strings of lights illuminating them as vacation-goers all enjoy their time.

"Want to go grab a drink?" I ask, pointing toward one of the bars down at the beach.

"Sure, but let's go drop off my stuff first, since we're only a block or so away from the condo."

We do just that, dropping off the bag before heading back out and across the street to the beach bar.

"Good evening, what can I get the two of you tonight?" the bartender asks as we approach.

"I'll take a beer. Do you have anything local on tap? And Ren, what would you like?" I ask, turning in Lauren's direction as she slides up to the bar next to me.

"I'll take Malibu Sunset, please," she tells the bartender.

"We have the 30A Beach Blonde Ale on tap, if you'd like to try it," the bartender tells me.

"I'll give it a try."

"Did you guys want to open a tab or pay by the drink?"

"Let's open a tab," I tell him, dropping my credit card on the bar.

A few moments later, he sets down Lauren's drink and my beer, and returns my credit card to me. "Just flag me down when you need a refill or something else."

"Thank you," Lauren and I reply as he steps down the bar to help another customer.

We grab our drinks and make our way closer to the beach, finding a small empty table to sit down, at the edge of the wood flooring.

"Any ideas on what we should do tomorrow?" I ask, after trying my beer.

"I was looking at a website that lists a bunch of the fun things to do down here. I was thinking we could go rent a pair of bicycles and ride along all the little shopping areas. They listed a few places along the way that have mini golf and more food trucks, music stages, things like that. I'm also happy with just hanging down at the beach or at the condo some, too."

"The bikes sound like a good idea. Did the website say where we can find the rental spot at?"

"It looked like the rental spots are all over, but I can look up for sure where the closest one is."

We finish our drinks, just as a band starts to set up just down on the sand off the bar.

"Did you want another drink? We can stay and listen to the band, or head back to the condo."

"I could go for one more drink."

"Same thing, or did you want something different?" I ask, standing and grabbing our empty glasses.

"Same, please," she tells me.

I head back to the bar, flagging down the bartender who helped us before, and order our drinks. He quickly gets them made and I'm back to the table, drinks in hand, within minutes.

The band strikes up as I sit down, and Lauren starts dancing in her seat.

"Would you like to hit the dance floor?" I ask, offering her my hand.

"Sure!" she squeals, taking my hand, and I lead her onto the dance floor.

We dance and enjoy ourselves over the next hour or so, just letting everything go and appreciating the music and atmosphere. The dance floor is a popular place and the band is really good. They play a good mix of covers as well as some of their own original music.

"I need another drink!" Lauren yells in my ear over the noise of the crowd, nodding toward the bar. I grab her hand and lead us through the crowd and up to the bar.

"What can I get ya?" the bartender asks.

"Can I get an ice water and a Malibu Sunset?" Ren asks.

"Sure, and for you, sir?" she asks me.

"I'll take a water and a glass of the 30A Beach Blonde Ale you have on tap. We have an open tab as well, that you can put these on."

"What's the name for the tab?"

"Sam Cole."

"Here're your waters. Just give me a minute and I'll have your drinks up," she tells us as she steps away to start making them.

"Did you want to stay here longer, or are you ready to call it a night?" I ask Lauren as we wait for the bartender to return with our drinks, having already sucked down our glasses of water.

"I think I'm ready to call it a night after we finish off the drinks we just ordered. Dancing wore me out!" she says, smiling at me.

"It was a lot of fun. We'll have to come back and check this place out again this week."

The bartender approaches with our drinks and sets them on the bar top in front of us. "Can I get you guys anything else?"

"You can close out the tab when you have a moment, we're ready to call it a night."

"No problem, I'll go grab your slip now."

I turn so I'm facing Lauren, but looking toward the band. I watch as the crowd dances along to the song they're currently playing.

"Thanks for tonight. It's just what I needed," Lauren tells me, pulling my attention back to her.

"Anytime, Ren." I reach out to cup her cheek, wiping an eyelash off.

The small smile she gives me, the one that's always been just for me, sends a jolt straight to my heart and my dick. I don't know how I'm going to hold in my self-control and let her set the pace on whatever this is between us, but I know I have to.

18

LAUREN

THE PAST COUPLE OF DAYS HAS BEEN EVERYTHING. THE TIME away to decompress was just what I needed, and the added bonus of spending all that time alone with Sam was a *very* added bonus. We spent many hours down at the beach, swam a little, explored the area on bikes, and stopped and played mini-golf at a few different places. We listened to so much music along the beach, as well as eating and drinking our way up and down the boardwalk. I'm actually sad to be leaving this morning, but Sam has to get me back so that he can go back home. Work calls for him in just a couple days.

"Do you need help loading anything in the car?" Sam hollers from another room.

I walk out to find him, having just finished zipping up my suitcase.

"I just finished packing, so if you want to load this up, you can."

"Sure, can you do a look through on my room, just to make sure I didn't miss anything? I can do the same with yours if you'd like."

"Yep, and then I'll double-check the bathroom."

"Sounds good. Be right back," he says, grabbing my suitcase and heading for the car.

I do my walk through of his room, the bathroom, kitchen, and living room areas, not finding anything left behind.

"Just my room left to check as I've done all the other rooms. Then we can hit the road."

"Okay, I'll check it quick if you want to go get loaded up."

OUR ROAD TRIP BACK IS UNEVENTFUL, AND WE SWITCH ON AND off driving each time we stop to stretch and use the bathroom or grab something to eat. The conversation between the two of us has been so easy this past week and we've talked about so much, but still haven't defined what we want between the two of us, and when. I know I need to take time for myself and just be me, but I also don't want to waste any more time not being together. Then comes the other issue of us living hundreds of miles apart.

With about an hour left until we make it back, I reach over and turn the radio down so that we can talk a little more seriously without the distraction.

"So, what are we doing? I know you said you'd wait for me to be ready for more, and I still think I need that. I still need to take some time for myself, but I also don't want to waste any more time either."

"I'm willing to go at your pace, Ren. But I also think it's a good idea if you take some time for yourself. It also isn't like we can see each other everyday right now. So, we'll have to rely on calling, texting, and FaceTiming when we can.

Depending on what case I get assigned to when I get back will determine my availability. Big cases can sometimes take up most of my time while we're in the depths of solving it."

"Do you think, once you're home and find out your case load, I could possibly come visit you for a few days or long weekend before school starts back up for me in August?"

"Absolutely! Even if I'm assigned to a case, I can probably get a couple days off. You pick the dates and I'll make it happen."

"And what happens if we do this, and then realize that we're better off as just friends?"

"Then we'd know we gave it a try, and if friends is all we're supposed to be, then we'll be the best of friends. No hard feelings."

"And this isn't going to be weird for you and Steven?"

"Don't worry about me and Steven, Ren. He's known for years how I feel about you, and has been pushing me to tell you. I'm sure he will be perfectly fine with whatever we decide is best for the two of us."

"Okay. I just don't want anything to come between you two. I'd hate myself if I was the cause of something."

"Lauren, seriously, don't worry about Steven and me. You aren't going to come between us. We're good. He's good with us, and would support us no matter what we decide is best for the two of us. I might be your brother's best friend, but he has to share that spot with you. Even with all the distance between us, I've never not considered you my best friend and I hope that never changes," Sam tells me, the vulnerability noticeable in his voice.

"Okay, then I won't worry," I assure him. He reaches over and grabs my hand, linking our fingers, and gives my hand a gentle squeeze.

"We do this, at your pace. Whatever that is. Got it?"

I can't help the huge smile that fills my face at his words.

"Yes, I got it," I tell him before I lean over and kiss his cheek.

19

SAM

THE PAST SIX WEEKS HAVE FLOWN BY. AS SOON AS I RETURNED from Kentucky, I was thrown into a big case that has kept me so busy I forget what day it is most of the time. I, however, *don't* forget that Lauren will be arriving this afternoon and will be staying with me for the next five days.

Five days alone with her.

Five days of her in my bed—hopefully naked. Hey, I'm a man, and a horny one at that.

Five days to see if this is going to work between us.

Five days to be as normal a couple as we can be.

"Sam, you there?" Jennings says, waving his hand in front of my face.

"Sorry, zoned out there for a minute."

Dave Jennings is one of the other agents based out of my home office. We became friends when we both started at this office the same day; me, as a brand-new agent and him, as a transfer. He'd been with the Bureau for about eighteen months when he was transferred to this location. We've been good friends ever since.

He just laughs at me. "How long until she arrives?"

"I need to leave for the airport in about thirty minutes."

He laughs at me again. "So, I'll see you again in, what, six days?"

"Yep, don't expect to see me before that, unless you and Meg want to grab dinner one night."

"I'm sure we could make that happen. Just text me. About time we meet the famous Lauren. That is, if you let her out of your bed long enough," he ribs me.

"I've got to get her into it first, before I can even think about letting her leave it," I grumble. We haven't discussed the whole intimacy aspect of what we both expect to happen this week. I'd never expect nor pressure her into it, but that doesn't lessen the fact that I'm a man and she is the woman I want. That, and I only have a one-bedroom condo, that only has one bed. So, unless I sleep on the couch, she's going to be in my arms each night and that body against mine is going to have my dick hard all the time.

If how steamy some of our phone and video chat sessions have gotten over the past few weeks is any indication, I don't think we'll be keeping our hands off each other much this trip.

"You think any more about putting in for that transfer to the Kentucky office?"

"Yeah, I actually submitted my request this morning. I was going to surprise Lauren with that information once she gets here."

"Well, keep me posted on that. I'll hate to see you go, but understand why you want to."

"Thanks, man, I just need to be near her if this is ever going to work long-term, and I know that she doesn't want to leave home. Plus, she's at such a great school, so I'd hate to ask her to move here."

I STAND AT THE EXIT FOR SECURITY, MY BACK AGAINST A PILLAR and hands stuffed in my pockets as I watch the steady stream of people. Lauren texted me about ten minutes ago, letting me know she'd touched down but was still taxiing to the gate, and that she'd see me soon.

I finally see her in the crowd as she makes her way down the hall and out to the open. I watch as she scans the area looking for me, and when our eyes meet, the smile that fills her face causes me to replicate hers. She saunters over to me, dropping her carry-on at my feet, and then launches herself into my arms, burying her face in my neck. I nuzzle the crook of her neck as I hold her tight against me.

"I missed you so damn much," I mumble into her neck, placing an open-mouthed kiss against her skin. The shiver that runs through her body doesn't go unnoticed. She pulls back, and drops her forehead to mine, as we make eye contact.

"I missed you, too," she whispers.

I squeeze her once more, then slide her down my body. No way could she miss the erection in my jeans.

"Let's go grab your luggage so we can get out of here," I tell her, placing a kiss on her forehead. I reach down and grab her carry-on bag, and then her hand, as we walk toward baggage claim.

Thankfully, the luggage from her flight is already coming out when we find the carousel, and quickly locate her bag. We head straight for my truck parked out in the lot.

"Are you hungry?" I ask, once we're in the truck and pulling out of the airport.

"Getting there. Did you have plans yet for dinner tonight?"

"I figured I'd grill us some steaks, and I picked up some twice baked potatoes from the store, as well as some salad fixings."

"That all sounds so good," she tells me as I reach over and place my hand on her bare knee, giving it a little squeeze. The cut-off shorts she's got on don't leave much to the imagination and fuck, does she look hot in them.

"I'm happy you're here," I tell her. "I'm excited to show you around, maybe even introduce you to a few of my friends while you're here, if you're up to it."

"Of course! I want to see everything and meet the people here that are important to you. Do I get to see where you work? Is that allowed?"

"Yes, I can take you in and show you where I work." I chuckle. "I might work for the FBI, but I can still take you around and tell you a little bit about my work."

"I'm excited to see where it is you work all day. Where it is you catch criminals," she says excitedly.

I just laugh at her excitement as we drive to my house. I've been looking forward to this visit since she first asked about coming to visit me on our way home from the beach trip.

We make it to my condo about fifteen minutes later, and I grab her suitcase as she grabs her carry-on bag. I lead her inside, dropping her stuff off in my room, and give her the quick tour of the place.

My place isn't huge, but it's not small either, around a thousand square feet, and it's the traditional bachelor pad. I have a huge flat-screen TV taking up one wall in the living room that can be seen from just about everywhere, except the bathroom and my bedroom.

"Can I get you something to drink? I've got beer, and I

picked up some of your favorite wine. I also have pop, and water?"

"A glass of wine sounds perfect. Did you need help getting dinner started?" she offers.

"Sure, let me go fire up the grill. Can you grab the food from the fridge in the meantime?"

"Yep, do I need to season up the steaks?"

"Yes, please. The seasonings are in the cabinet to the left of the stove. Feel free to use any of them."

I step out on the balcony and before I can fire up the grill, I have to change out the propane tank. With the new one installed, I fire it up and get it warming.

"Grill should be ready in just a couple of minutes." I step back inside, where Lauren is in my kitchen, finishing up the steaks. I step up behind her and wrap an arm around her torso, bringing my lips down to her exposed neck, where I drop my lips. "Thanks for getting those ready," I say against her skin, which pebbles against my lips.

Lauren squirms, causing her ass to grind against me, which has my dick hardening in my jeans.

"You might want to stop that if you want to eat anytime soon," I warn her, and she stills against me.

"Is that so?" she sassily says, as she grinds her ass against me once more.

I spin her in my arms so fast a gasp escapes her lips. Her arms come up and circle around my neck as she sinks her fingers in the hair at the back of my neck.

It's been a long time since I've held a woman in my arms like this. The desire is so thick between the two of us. Lauren and I had a few moments that could have turned into something more when we were at the beach, but we both controlled ourselves, knowing she needed time. But now, fuck, I don't think we're going to be able to make it past tonight without tearing each other's clothes off.

"Unless you tell me to stop, I'm going to kiss you now," I tell her, cupping her cheeks with my hands. I bring my face closer to hers, angling her face, pausing just slightly, giving her another chance to tell me to stop.

When she doesn't make a sound, nor pull away from me, I finally, *finally,* bring my lips to hers. A moan bubbles up from deep within her chest, and I just swallow it right up, pulling her as close to my body as I can with the barrier of clothes between the two of us. It only takes one swipe of my tongue against her lips for her to open up to me, and I lick my way into her mouth.

Our tongues caress as I deepen the kiss. Time stands still as the kiss goes on, neither one of us wanting it to end. The light tug of the hairs on the back of my neck has tingles sliding down my back and not stopping until they reach my balls. My dick is straining against the zipper so hard that I'll probably have an imprint of it for days.

We finally break our connection, both gulping in air as our foreheads come together.

"T-t-that was intense," Lauren stammers out, her fingers coming up to rest against her lips.

"Best first kiss."

"Yeah," she agrees.

"I should probably get the food on the grill, I'm sure it's hot enough now."

"Yeah, let me help you carry everything out," she offers. Before I take a step back, I drop a chaste kiss on her lips one more time, needing another taste of them.

We both grab a plate of food and walk outside. I lift the lid of the grill and place the steaks on, then the foil wrapped potatoes and the veggies. After adjusting the heat settings, I close the lid and step over to the small table and chairs I have out here. While I placed the food on the grill, Lauren stepped back inside and grabbed our drinks and brought them out.

"Thanks," I say as she hands me my open beer, and I drop another kiss onto her lips. Now that I've tasted her once, I'm never going to get enough, and I'm already dreading when I have to take her back to the airport next week.

"You're welcome," she says, smiling against my lips, and then I kiss her again.

20

LAUREN

THE DINNER THAT SAM MADE US WAS DELICIOUS. HE MANAGED to not burn it between kissing me constantly, not that I would have complained if he did, because man, can he kiss. Those lips could get me into trouble if I'm not careful this week.

We end up eating out on the deck, as we had a nice breeze helping cool us off slightly. I enjoy another glass of wine with dinner as Sam has another beer with his.

"Did you have any plans yet for tomorrow?" I ask, as I sit back and sip my wine.

"The morning should be the coolest part of the day, so if you wanted to get out and do a little hiking, that would be the best time to do so. There are a few places around here that have nice trails that I think you'd enjoy."

"Sounds like the perfect morning."

"Then maybe in the afternoon, I can take you to my work and show you around, introduce you to a few of my coworkers."

"Sounds like a good plan," I say, a yawn escaping from my lips.

"Are you ready to call it a night?" Sam asks, as he sets his empty beer bottle down on the table.

"I think so. Between the flying and the wine, I'm exhausted."

"Well then, let's get you to bed," he says, standing and collecting some of the items on the table. I grab the remaining plates and carry them into the kitchen. We both quickly work together to get all the dishes loaded in the dishwasher. Once it's loaded, Sam locks up and we head to the bedroom.

"I only have the one bed, so if you'd prefer I sleep on the couch, I will."

I walk over to stand right in front of him, not leaving much space between the two of us. I run my hands up his firm chest and wrap them around his neck as his hands land on my hips.

"That won't be necessary," I tell him, lifting up on my toes to press my lips to his. He quickly takes control of the kiss and deepens it. His hands slide down to cup my ass and lift me up. I immediately wrap my legs around his waist as the kiss continues on and deepens even more.

By the time we break our connection, I'm sucking in much-needed air.

I slide down Sam's body, not missing his hard muscles or the bulge in his jeans. I want nothing more than to feel his skin against mine. Feel him inside of me. He's talked me through a few orgasms over the phone, and I'm ready to experience one—*or a hundred*—at the mercy of his body, not just his words.

"I'll be back in just a few seconds," I tell him, pushing up to drop a quick kiss against his stubble-covered cheek.

I grab my bathroom bag and the sexy nightie I brought with me for just this purpose. I close the bathroom door behind me, flipping the lock to make sure he stays out while I change and get ready for bed. It only takes me a few minutes to finish up, and before I head out, I stop and take a few deep breaths. Once I feel calm and confident, I unlock and open the door. I flip off the light and walk out full of confidence toward the bed. He's sitting on the edge, having stripped down to his boxer briefs and sweet baby Jesus, is he sex-on-a-stick.

"Hi," I shyly say, grabbing his attention.

The look on his face as he takes me in turns from calm-cool-collected to wanton desire and lust filling his facial features.

"Fuck," he whispers. "Y-y-you look fucking amazing. Get over here."

He holds his hand out to me. I close the small amount of space between us, and once I'm within his reach, he wraps his arm around my waist and pulls me into him. I'm standing between his legs as his head rests just between my breasts. We stay in this position for a few moments, no words being spoken.

Sam drops open-mouthed kisses along the opening of the nightie, and up onto the exposed tops of my breasts. He's keeping his lips to exposed skin, and I encourage him to explore the covered skin when I reach up and pull the tie between my breasts that is holding the flimsy material together. As soon as the tie is undone, it slips to the sides and exposes my full breasts to him. My nipples are already hard, and I long to feel his mouth on them.

Sam looks up at me; the look of longing and desire is intoxicating and has my body zinging with desire also.

He pulls my face down to his, locking his lips on my own. I fall into him, straddling him as he pulls me up onto his lap.

The kiss is hot, and neither of us can get enough of each other. His lips eventually leave my own, tracking a path across my jaw and down my neck. The scruff on his face tickles my sensitive skin as he moves, causing me to squirm and laugh.

Sam pulls away from me, looking up with a smile filling his face. "What's so funny?"

"Your beard is tickling me," I say, as I rub my hands against his cheeks.

"Like this?" he asks, dropping his chin to rub it against my collarbone.

"Yes!" I shriek and try to squirm away, but he tightens his hold and continues to torture me.

My shrieks turn to a moan when his lips wrap around my left nipple and suck hard. His tongue flicks against my hardened peak as he teases me, lightly nipping with his teeth and causing a rush of wetness to pool between my thighs.

"Holy, yes!" I pant, running my hands in his hair as I hold his head against my breast. He releases the suction and kisses his way over to my other breast, showing it equal attention. By the time he latches his lips around my right breast, my hips have started to grind against his erection. I can feel my desire soaking my thong and now his boxers.

"God, you feel amazing," he says against my breast. "I can already feel how ready you are for me."

He drops his hand down and between my legs, stroking his fingers along my seam, teasing my clit over the barrier of the fabric. He finally slips my thong to the side and his skin makes contact with mine. His touch has me just about cresting over the edge of orgasm and as soon as he sinks two fingers inside my pussy, my body starts clenching his fingers as I crest over the edge. I ride out my orgasm on his hand as he kisses from my breasts up to my lips.

"That's it, baby, take it. Fuck my fingers and take what you need. You're so goddamned beautiful when you come," he whispers into my ear as I fall.

My hips come to a stop as I completely collapse against him, effectively knocking us back in the bed so he's flat on his back with me sprawled on top of him. His hands rub up and down my back as I come down from the intensity of my orgasm. If he's able to have me falling that hard just from his mouth and fingers, I'm a little scared what will happen when he has me coming while he's inside me.

Once I've gathered a little of my strength back, I roll off of him, removing the nightie completely, and curl up at his side.

"That was intense," I finally tell him.

"We're just getting started," he says, dropping a kiss on the tip of my nose before he flips me on my back and hovers over me. The smirk on his face sends tingles through my body once again as I watch his eyes drag up and down my body.

"You're perfect. You know that?" he says, dragging his lips from my belly button up my torso, past my breasts and to my collarbone.

"Mhmmm..." I moan, then bring his lips to mine, locking them together, allowing him to take control of the kiss. He grinds his dick against my center, causing me to break the kiss as I gasp in pure pleasure.

"I need you inside of me," I pant into his ear, nipping at the lobe.

"Don't worry, sweetheart, we'll get there in due time." He smirks at me.

"Ughhh." I mock pout, and he just laughs at me, so I

reach down and slip my hand inside his briefs. I stroke his cock, making sure I run my fingertip over his seam.

"Fuuuuck." He moans.

"Don't make me wait, Sam," I tell him, not showing him any sympathy in my rhythm as I continue stroking him. With my free hand, I push his briefs off his hips then down his legs as best I can from the angle I'm at. I finally get a look at him naked and fuck me, he's the perfect male specimen.

He stands and kicks his briefs to the side, then grabs his cock with his hand and gives it a few tugs. He slips his hands up my legs until he reaches the strings along my hips and pulls the thong from my body. The sexy swagger that he possesses in this moment is such a fucking turn-on that I can't keep myself from whimpering slightly as my thong clears my feet and he takes in my naked body.

"Condom?" he asks.

"Yes, I'm not on birth control, remember. I can't be," I tell him. Due to a clotting issue I have, I can't be on traditional hormonal birth control.

"I remember. Just making sure we're on the same page here, Ren." He reaches over to his nightstand and pulls out a brand-new box. Opening it, he pulls out the string of condoms and tears a few of the packages apart, tossing one on the bed next to me and the others on the nightstand.

I grab the package he tossed next to me and tear it open. I sit up on the bed and with him now standing between my own legs, I dip down and wrap my lips around the head of his cock. The angle isn't great, so I slide down the edge of the bed, needing a better angle to suck his cock into the back of my throat. The noises falling from his lips are reassurance that he's enjoying this impromptu blowjob.

Not wanting him to come in my mouth this time, I bob my head up and down his length only a few times before I pop off and roll the condom down his length, then slide back up on the bed.

The nerves hit me that I'm about to have sex with Sam. The man I've loved since I was a little girl. The boy who was my best friend for so many years. The one who I have some of the best memories in my entire life with.

The nerves flee my body when Sam hovers over me and brings his lips to mine again.

"Are you ready?" he whispers against my lips as he rubs the head of his cock up and down my center, making sure to tease my clit, causing me to squirm under him.

"Y-yes," I answer him.

"Keep your eyes on me, Ren. I feel like I've waited a life-time for this moment, and I want to look at you."

With our eyes locked, I feel the head of his cock pressing against my entrance, and then he slowly pushes past as he sinks in until he's balls deep.

The tightness and fullness I feel once he's fully seated is overwhelming, and I bite his exposed neck. He stills, allowing me time to adjust to his size.

"You feel so perfect, all tight around my cock." He pulls out until just the tip remains, and then he slams back into me. "I love you, Ren," he says, as he quickly finds a rhythm that has us both building quickly to our climax. I move my legs and bring them up, so my feet are resting on his shoulders, which changes the angle in which he hits me inside, and that has me falling over the crest once again.

"Yes!" I cry out. "Please don't stop."

He pounds into me now at a frantic pace as he works to chase his own release. I can feel his cock swell inside me, and the warmth of his cum filling the condom has my body clenching around him again in an aftershock.

Sam collapses, his body against mine, but his weight still on his own arms.

"That was fucking perfect. Give me about twenty to rebound, and we'll do it all over again," he says as he pulls out of me and quickly removes the condom, tying it off before tossing it in the trash next to his bed.

21

SAM

I WAKE UP EARLY, LAUREN ASLEEP CURLED UP IN MY ARMS. SHE'S spooned in front of me, both of us on our sides. With one hand resting on her lower abdomen and the other cupping her breast, I don't think I could wake up in a better position. My dick is hardening as the moments pass by with our bodies so close. I drop my lips to her shoulder and pepper it with kisses. Last night was hands-down the best night I've ever had. Sinking inside her for the first time was so much better than I could have ever dreamed it to be. Her body was so responsive to mine, and I could feel her come alive with each stroke of my cock and touch of my fingers as I claimed her body, claimed her heart and soul.

It didn't fail to go unnoticed that she didn't return my proclamation of love last night, but in all honesty, I didn't expect her to. I know we've grown closer these past couple months, and while I know she loves me, I also realize she may not be ready to say it out loud. I don't mind, though. I told her I'd wait for as long as it takes, and I intend to keep that promise.

I ease my body away from hers, doing my best not to

wake her as I slip out of bed. I grab a clean pair of briefs from my dresser, carrying them into the bathroom with me. I quickly use the bathroom, slip my briefs on, then wash my hands and brush my teeth. I head out into the kitchen and get the coffee started. I pour two cups, adding cream to Lauren's cup, and then carry them back to the bedroom. I set down the cups on my end table and just take in her being in my bed.

Her hair is wild and surrounds her face on the pillow. She has the sheet pulled up to her chin, but her back is exposed from where I was pressed against her. I can see the swell of her breasts and it has me hardening again. We made love three times throughout the night, so I know she's tired and needs to sleep.

I abandon the coffee and crawl back in bed, sliding right back into my vacated spot. After getting situated, I drift back off to sleep with her in my arms.

I WAKE A FEW HOURS LATER TO AN EMPTY BED. THE SHEETS next to me are cold, so I know Lauren has been up for a while, or at least long enough for them to go cold. I hop out of bed, needing to find her, wanting to have her back in my arms.

I walk out to the living room and find her curled up on the couch in my t-shirt and a blanket draped over her lap. She's got a cup of hot coffee in one hand and her kindle in the other. She looks so perfect sitting there on my couch, wearing my clothes. I can perfectly envision this exact moment for years to come.

"Mornin'," I call out, the sleep still evident in my voice.

She sets her kindle down on her lap as she looks up at me. "Morning, how'd you sleep?"

"Good, until I woke up without you next to me." I make my way over to her, dropping to sit on the coffee table so I can face her. I place my lips against hers, getting that morning kiss I now crave. Kissing her is like my drug, and I'm now an addict, looking for my next hit.

"Did you get up earlier? There was coffee in the pot already when I got up."

"Yeah, I woke up and made a pot, but when I went back into the room, you looked so peaceful sleeping that I just curled back up with you and fell back asleep."

"You should have woken me up. I would have kept you company," she says, a coy smile flashing across her lips.

"Is that so?" I state, dropping another kiss to her lips.

"Yep," she says, popping the P.

"Did you still want to go on a hike this morning?"

"Sure, I'm up for just about anything."

"Anything?" I ask, raising my eyebrows at her with a mischievous look on my face.

"Get your mind out of the gutter, Sam," she chides, laughter filling her voice. "You're such a guy."

"You weren't complaining about that fact last night," I remind her.

"Oh, shut it." She slaps me in the chest before she slides her hand up to rub my beard. I don't usually grow a beard for more than a couple of days, but with the way she responds to it, I might just be keeping the facial hair around.

"Never," I reply, capturing her lips again.

I pull back reluctantly, contrary to either of our desires. "Let's go get showered and dressed. We can then grab some breakfast and get out and hit the trails."

"Would you like to shower with me? Save water and all

that?" Lauren asks, the hunger she has for me apparent in her voice as she stands from the couch, and that's when I realize she's only got on my t-shirt. No thong or panties, just my fucking shirt.

Wet-fucking-dream.

AFTER A VERY LONG SHOWER THAT HAD US BOTH COMING apart at each other's hands, we finally got dressed and left the house for our hike and visit to my office.

We take the trail I choose at a leisurely pace. We walk it the entire way, hand in hand, neither of us wanting to be very far from each other, loving the feel of our skin touching. We stop along the way, to snap a few pictures of the views as well as a selfie of the two of us.

"How about we grab some lunch before we stop at my work?"

"Sounds perfect. Did you want to go somewhere or head back to the condo?"

"I'm fine with either, what would you prefer?" I ask.

"Your choice. I'll let you surprise me."

"We can hit up this little deli near my work. They have some of the best sandwiches you'll ever taste."

We hop back in my truck and I drive us over. I park in the secured lot for my work, and we walk the couple of blocks over to the deli. We enter, and the line is a few people deep, which isn't surprising to me at all. This place can get crazy busy almost daily.

We make it to the front of the line and after placing our order, we find a place to sit and wait for our lunch.

"Do you come here a lot?" Lauren asks me once we sit down at a table for two.

"Yep, probably a few times a week. It's quick and easy to get here. Plus, we can call in an order and they will get it all ready for us. That, and I've probably tried everything on the menu, and never once had something I didn't like."

"BLT, with potato salad?" an employee says, standing next to our table.

"Right here," I tell the girl as she sets my food down in front of me.

"And a Club sandwich with a side of slaw," she says to Lauren.

"Thank you," we say together, as the young girl grabs the table marker we got when we placed our order, and walks off.

"Holy cow, this looks amazing," Lauren says, looking down at her plate. "You weren't kidding when you said the portions were huge. I don't think I'll be able to even eat half of this."

"Eat what you can, and we can take the rest with us," I state, picking up my sandwich to take a huge bite.

We each dig in, enjoying our lunch and the easy conversation that flows between the two of us. With only being able to communicate the past few weeks via talking, texting, and video chatting, we've returned back to the easiness we had when we were younger. I no longer feel like there's this huge distance between us, and after last night, I can only hope that feeling never returns.

"Ready to go check out my office?" I ask as we box up our leftovers and head out of the deli.

"Yep. Can we drop this off in the truck first?"

"That was my plan," I say as Lauren slips her hand in mine as we walk down the street.

We quickly drop the bag in my truck and make our way inside the building. We have to enter through the main front doors, so that I can get Lauren signed in and a visitor badge. It only takes a few minutes to do so and we're quickly riding the elevator up to my department.

We exit the elevator and are greeted by the receptionist for the floor, Becky.

"Agent Cole, nice to see you today," she greets us. "And who's this lovely young lady with you?"

"Becky, I'd like for you to meet my girlfriend, Lauren. Lauren, this is Becky. She keeps this department running and all of us agents in line," I state. Becky is like the mom of this department. She's worked here for twenty some-odd years, and knows more than I ever will about working for the agency.

"Nice to meet you, Lauren. Nice to see someone is keeping this guy in line when he isn't here at work." She winks at the both of us.

"Nice to meet you, too."

"Is Jennings in?" I ask Becky.

"Should be, his light is showing he's in the office, and I don't know of any agent meetings taking place today."

"Thanks, we'll see you on the way out," I tell her as I escort Lauren through the secured doors and down the hall.

We pass by some empty conference rooms before the hall opens up to a large room.

"This is the bullpen," I explain, motioning to the big open room with computer stations in some areas, a large projection screen where we can pull up all kinds of information, and a large conference table for when we have a big case with many hands-on deck. "We gather in here, looking over all kinds of data, as we work to solve the case. Briefings happen in this room, as well."

Since no big cases are currently being worked on today,

the bullpen is pretty sparse. I escort Lauren through the bullpen and to my office.

"This is my space," I tell her, opening the door and flipping on the light.

"It's very you," she muses, looking up at me with a sparkle in her eye.

"How so?" I ask.

"Just the little personal touches," she says, sitting down in my desk chair. She sees the picture I have framed of the two of us from our trip to the beach, reaching out to pick it up, and she smiles. It was a candid selfie I'd snapped one day while we'd been riding bikes around town. We're smiling at the camera, both happy and carefree in that moment.

"I completely forgot you took this," she tells me, setting the picture back down.

"I have others, but that was my favorite," I tell her, taking a seat in one of my visitors' chairs.

"Knock-knock," I hear Jennings say as he thumps on the door frame and steps into the office. "Couldn't stay away, huh, man?"

"Lauren wanted to come check out where it is I work all day."

"Ah! Lauren, since this guy doesn't seem to have any manners, it's nice to meet you. I'm Dave Jennings."

"Nice to meet you, Dave," she says, accepting the hand he offered to her.

"Don't be a jackass." I smack him in the chest. "I would have introduced you if you hadn't barged your way in here," I say on a laugh.

"We still doing dinner one night while she's in town? Meg would love to meet Lauren and see you," he says.

I look to Lauren, who smiles and shrugs, ultimately leaving the decision up to me.

"Yep, what night works for you? We don't have any concrete plans yet for the rest of her stay."

"Doesn't matter to me. I don't think we have anything going on, but I'll send Meg a text just to verify and get back to you."

"Sounds good, just let me know when you hear back from her."

"Will do, and it was nice to meet you, Lauren."

"Nice to meet you, too. I've heard good things about you and look forward to meeting your wife," Lauren tells him as he turns to walk out of my office. "He seems nice," she adds, after he leaves the office, and I grin at her.

"Yep, one of the nicest guys I know. You'll love his wife," I reply. "Want to continue our tour?" I ask, bending down to kiss her lips.

"Sure," she says breathlessly. I didn't even kiss her that deep, wanting to keep things PG, since we *are* at my work and all. Though, I wouldn't mind bending her over my desk and having my way with her.

I grab her hand and pull her up, linking our fingers once she's standing. I shut off the light in my office before pulling the door closed behind us, and we walk down the hall to some of the other agents' offices. I introduce her to everyone we come into contact with before we head back to the front to check out with Becky. No one gets in or out of this department without Becky knowing.

22

LAUREN

We leave Sam's work and head back to his condo, and as we're pulling in, he gets a text from Dave, saying that they are free tonight, if we want to get together for dinner.

"Does that sound okay to you?" he asks me as he parks his truck in his garage.

"Yep, I'm fine with whatever."

He shoots off a text, letting Dave know we're good with tonight, and at Meg's insistence, we make plans to go to their house.

Sam grabs our bag of leftovers and we head inside. I go straight for the bathroom and Sam stops in the kitchen to put our food in the fridge.

I wander out to the living room to find him on the couch, so I walk over to stand in front of him. He pulls me down so I'm sitting on his lap.

"Did you enjoy yourself today?" he asks, dropping a kiss on my neck.

"Yes, I like knowing where it is you work all those long hours being a badass computer guy."

He just laughs at my description of him.

"I also really enjoyed our hike this morning. It was beautiful out there."

"It sure was. Did you want to do anything before we head over to Dave and Meg's in a few hours?"

"Do you have any baking ingredients? I'd like to make a dessert to bring with us."

He just gives me a blank stare. "Um, babe. If you haven't noticed, I've been a bachelor for a long time. I don't even think I have flour or sugar, not to mention any other baking ingredients. But we can run up to the store and pick some up, or grab an already made dessert."

"Let me check if you even have the correct type of pan, and then I'll decide if it's worth buying all the ingredients to make something versus buying something."

"Whatever you want," he says, before turning my face so he can kiss me on the lips.

I pull back after a few moments and drop my head to his shoulder.

"I could kiss you forever," he tells me, placing a kiss to my temple.

I relax further into Sam, his arms coming around me as he pulls me tighter against him. Neither one of us make any effort to move from this spot.

"What are you busy thinking about?" he asks.

"Not really thinking, just enjoying being here with you. Enjoying what little time we have together on this trip," I tell him honestly.

Sam picks me up off his lap, then shifts so he can lie on his side on the couch and pulls me back down to mirror his position.

"I'm glad you came," he whispers against my lips once we're both situated, lying face to face.

"Me too," I reply, linking my arms around his neck and

sinking my fingers into his hair as I play with the short hairs at the nape of his neck.

"Mhmm. I love it when you do that."

"Do what?"

"Run your fingers through my hair like that. It does things to me," he growls, before dropping his lips to my neck. His scruff tickles my sensitive skin, causing me to squirm as it turns me on even more.

"Sam," I moan.

"Yes, Ren," he rumbles against my skin.

"What are you doing?"

He removes his lips from my skin and looks up at me with a devilish look on his face. "If you have to ask, then I'm not doing a good enough job showing you." He chuckles.

"Oh," I say. I can feel my cheeks reddening with embarrassment. "You were doing a good job, I just didn't know what your intentions were. Fuck, I'm making this awkward now."

Sam drops his head against my chest as he laughs at the situation. "No, you're not making it awkward at all, babe. Just comical. Now, if you don't mind, I'll get back to hopefully rocking your world," he says, pushing up so he can drop a kiss on my lips, effectively shutting me up.

WITH OUR LITTLE AFTERNOON SEXY TIME ON THE COUCH, WE successfully used up any opportunity we had for me to bake something to take with us tonight. So, with plans to stop at a bakery on our way, we eventually get up and get ready for our evening out with Sam's friends. I grab my cell to take with me into the bathroom, needing to respond to Zoey's texts before she sends a search party out to find me.

Lauren: Hi, sorry I haven't replied to your text sooner, but I made it here. Things are wonderful! Going so much better than I could have ever dreamed. I have so much to tell you when I get back. Just know he's taking VERY good care of me in ALL ways. 😊

Zoey: You whore! I knew it! Glad to hear all is well in lover land. Don't come back knocked up. 😂

I just laugh at Zoey's antics and set my phone down so I can get ready to go.

"You're glowing," Sam tells me as I walk out of the bathroom. I'd pinned part of my hair back to keep it from my face. It was a little messed up after our time on the couch earlier. "I like knowing I put that glow there," he adds, pulling me into his arms.

"Is that so?" I tease him after we break the kiss we both gravitated to. "How do you know you put it there?"

He drops his hands to my ass, grabbing a handful as he presses his already hard cock against my belly.

"Because it was my name you were screaming just a little bit ago," he says, nipping at my jaw.

"We better get out of here now before you start something you can't finish in time."

Groaning, Sam stops his exploration of my chin with his lips, and steps back, reaching down to adjust himself in his jeans. The bulge behind his zipper leaves little to the imagination, now that I know what's behind it. I smirk up at him, knowing exactly what's in store for us once we return home.

I grab my purse and we head out to the truck.

"Do you know if they have any allergies?" I ask as Sam pulls up to the bakery so I can pick out something.

"None that I know of," he tells me as he opens the door for me to walk in ahead of him.

We look at the selection of cakes, pies, and pastries, all making my mouth water as I peruse our options.

"I don't know what to choose," I muse. "Anything stand out to you?"

"The pies are kinda calling my name," he says.

"Okay, which one? Everything looks too good, I can't decide."

"How about that one?" he says, pointing to a mixed berry pie with a crumb topping.

"Perfect," I tell him, as we get the employee's attention, letting her know what pie we'd like boxed up.

About fifteen minutes later, Sam pulls into Dave and Meg's driveway. We both hop out and since the pie was sitting on my lap for the drive, I carry it up to the house.

Sam knocks a couple of times and then walks in. "Put all your clothes back on, we're here," he calls out, laughter filling his voice.

I follow him as we walk toward the kitchen, where we find Meg chopping what looks to be salad fixings.

"Hey, guys!" she greets us.

"Hi, Meg," Sam greets her, dropping a kiss to her cheek. "I'd like for you to meet Lauren. Lauren, this is the saint of a woman who puts up with Dave on a daily basis."

"It's so nice to finally meet you, we've heard so much about you," she says.

"All good, I hope. Otherwise, don't believe a word he's said," I reply.

"Oh, don't worry. This man only has good things to say about you." She winks at Sam.

"Where is Dave anyways?" Sam asks.

"He's out dealing with the grill. Can I get you guys something to drink? I've got beer, wine, pop, water, sangria, or I can make up a pitcher of margaritas."

"Sangria would be great," I tell her.

"I'll just grab a beer and go find Dave," Sam says.

"Where would you like this?" I ask, holding up the pie box.

"Oh, just over there on the counter is fine. Thank you for bringing it, you didn't need to do that."

"It was the least I could do. Thank you so much for having us over. I wanted to make something, but Sam doesn't have any baking things. I would have had to buy everything I needed, so bakery-made will have to do for tonight."

"Well, you did good picking. That bakery is one of the best in town."

I set the pie down on the counter, and she hands me a glass full of sangria. I take a sip, enjoying the cool liquid as it slides down my throat.

"Are you enjoying your visit so far? You just got in yesterday, correct?"

"Yes, and yes. I got in late afternoon yesterday, so we just had a relaxing evening in. This morning, we went out hiking, and then Sam showed me around his work. I've always wondered what it was like inside his office."

"Do you guys have any other plans for your time here?" Meg questions.

"Not really. We're just enjoying our time together, but also doing whatever sounds fun at the time."

"If you want to see the beach, you should get him to take you to the Outer Banks. It's beautiful out there."

"Thanks for the suggestion, I'll mention it to him."

"I figured we could eat out on the patio, if you want to head out and see what the guys are up to."

"Sure, can I help bring anything out for you?" I offer.

"If you want to grab the salad, I can bring the dishes out."

We bring out everything, getting the table set and ready, as Dave finishes grilling the food.

We all enjoy the conversation that flows so easily between the four of us as we eat. I tell as many embarrassing stories of Sam that I can think of from our childhood, at the encouragement of Dave. I love seeing what good friends he has here. But it also makes me realize just how much distance is between the two of us. For this relationship to work long-term, one of us is going to have to pack up and move to be with the other, and as great of a time I'm having here with him, I just don't know if I could move away from my family. I've never really lived away from where I grew up, but on the flip side, I don't know if I can stand living so far from Sam for much longer.

We sit around long after we finish eating dinner, the conversation continuing to flow. Sam and Dave talk about some of their past cases—or at least what they are allowed to tell us about them. I love seeing how animated Sam gets when he talks about his work. It is apparent he really enjoys what he does. I love the fact that he found his passion in life and chased his dream.

The sun has long ago set when we finally pack up and head back to Sam's condo. By the time we make it, I'm yawning and having a hard time keeping my eyes open.

"They loved you," Sam says, as we pull into his garage.

"I really liked them, it makes me happy that you have such good friends here."

"Dave's a good guy, one of the best. And Meg is one of a kind. They've been through a lot in the past few years, and when most people would have crumbled from the stress and disarray, they turned to each other and really leaned on each other, and have come out stronger from their grief."

"What happened?"

"They had a full-term stillbirth. One day, Meg realized she hadn't felt him move all day and went in as a precaution. When she got there, and they couldn't find the heartbeat, they immediately sent her for an ultrasound. That confirmed the baby's heart had stopped beating, and she was sent to the hospital to induce labor. It was a very hard time for the both of them, and was for more than a year after, as expected. The doctors couldn't confirm a reason why it happened, which was almost more devastating to them. Dave confided in me not too long ago that they're thinking of trying again soon. They are obviously just nervous about it."

"Oh my," I gasp. "I couldn't imagine the heartbreak they dealt with." A few tears roll down my cheeks at the devastation they went through.

"They both still have moments when the grief hits them, but they have worked through most of it with the help of a counselor, and as I said before, just leaning on each other and helping each other grieve."

We both get out of the truck and head inside, our moods a little somber from the heaviness of what Sam just told me.

"Hey now," Sam says, backing me up against the closed door and pinning me against it. He cups my face, wiping the remnants of the few tears that I shed. "Let's not let that get us down this evening. We had a great time, and I have plans for you tonight." His lips tip up in a cocky grin.

"Is that so?" I ask, looking up into his eyes.

"Mmmhmm," he says, before dropping his lips to mine. He pins me harder against the door, and I can feel his erection against my stomach as he presses against me.

Sam takes complete control of the kiss, angling my head to deepen it. His other hand drops down until he's cupping my ass, and pulls my leg up high on his hip, so he can grind against me.

He breaks the kiss, dropping his forehead to mine for a moment. "I'd fuck you right here if I had a condom on me, so let's move this to the bedroom." His gravelly voice sends chills down my body, straight to my clit.

He steps back from me, pulling me along with him toward the bedroom, smacking my ass as we walk. As soon as we reach the bedroom, he picks me up from behind and sets me on the bed, then drops his lips to the exposed skin of my cleavage.

"This top has been driving me fucking crazy all evening," he says between each open-mouthed kiss. "Every time you moved, I'd get a glimpse of more skin, and every time, that glimpse would make my dick that much harder."

I just smile and laugh at him, his scruff doing a good job of tickling my skin and driving me crazy at the same time.

23

SAM

LAUREN'S BODY IS SO RESPONSIVE TO EVERY SINGLE ONE OF MY touches, which is a good thing, considering I crave to touch her. I'm going to go through serious withdrawals when she leaves in just a few more days.

I kiss my way up, from the tops of her breasts, along the column of her neck, and then pull back. I push up so my arms are extended fully. The redness of her skin where my facial hair has teased her skin just makes me want to claim her body even more. She simply watches me as I scan her with my eyes, the evidence of what she does to my body evident by the large bulge in my jeans.

"Are you just going to stare, or are you going to do something?" she finally asks, breaking me out of my trance.

"Oh, don't you worry, I've got lots of plans," I say, winking at her.

She just laughs, and fuck, if the sound of her carefree laughter doesn't make me love her even more than I already do.

I stand up fully and pull her to a seated position so that I can reach down and pull her shirt off over her head. Once hers is removed, I reach behind my head and pull off my t-shirt one-handed over my head.

"Mmmm." She moans when my abs come into view.

"Like something you see?" I ask, noticing she's now biting her lower lip. "You might have a little drool there, babe."

She smacks my stomach with the back of her hand. "No I don't!" she shrieks, then wipes at her lips with her other hand, just in case.

"I was just teasing you." I laugh back at her.

She unbuckles my belt, then unbuttons my jeans before sliding the zipper down. I know she isn't intending to do this slowly, but I swear to God, it is taking her forever to get my jeans open and my dick out.

She finally gets them fully open and pushes them off my hips, taking my boxer briefs with them. My erection springs up and hits my stomach once it's released from its confines. Just as my underwear hits the floors around my ankles, she sinks to the floor in front of me and simultaneously licks the underside of my cock from the base to the tip, swirling her tongue around my inflamed head before wrapping her lips around the tip and sucking me in so deep, I hit the back of her throat seconds later.

"Fuck, Ren. That feels so good," I tell her, letting her know I'm enjoying everything she's doing to me. When she swallows around my dick, I nearly come unglued, and know I can't take the torture much longer if I'm going to be able to hold out and fuck her like I'd planned on tonight. Much more of her mouth on me, and I'll be coming down her throat.

"Ren, baby." I place my hands under her arms and pull her up. I slam my lips to hers, kissing her as hard as I can.

"Any more of that sweet mouth on my dick, and I wasn't going to last any longer," I tell her against her lips. The smile that fills her face is intoxicating.

I drop a hand to her jeans, unfastening them quickly and dropping them to the ground. She quickly steps out of them, her thong following seconds later. I reach around and unfasten the clasp of her bra, and it joins the clothes piling up on the floor.

With the two of us now completely naked, standing in front of each other, I reach over to the nightstand and grab a condom, making quick work of opening it and sheathing myself.

I motion for Lauren to lie back on the bed, and she does so, pushing back so she's centered on it. I take a moment before joining her, to take in her beauty. The way her hair has fallen to surround her looks almost like a halo. The flush from her arousal makes her even more beautiful to me.

I place a knee on the bed, then slide forward, placing a kiss just above her clit on her mound.

She cries out as my tongue grazes ever so lightly over her sensitive nub before I suck it hard between my lips. Her hips buck up, pressing my face against her center. I lap and suck at her, listening and learning what she likes and what drives her crazy, from the way her body responds to me. I slip two fingers inside her, quickly finding that magic spot inside that will make her come undone. It only takes a few moments of teasing for her body to start pulsing around my fingers, and her to yell my name as she falls over the edge, her orgasm ripping through her body.

I lap at her slowly as her body recovers, every few licks pulling a few more shivers from her as they cause mini orgasms to roll through her.

I finally take pity on her and kiss my way up her body. I make it to her lips and as I claim them with my own, I slide my dick inside her, instantly feeling it clamp around me like a vise grip.

"Holy shit, you're fucking tight tonight," I whisper against her lips as I still and allow her body a few moments to adjust to me.

"I think it's you," she mumbles in return, and I just chuckle against her lips.

I feel her body relax and I slowly start to pump my hips, sliding out until just the tip is left and then plunging back in until I'm balls deep. I continue to move, following her cues as I make sure to build her up to her next release. Our sexual relationship might be extremely new, but I'm learning very quickly what works and doesn't work for her. I know now that if I work hard enough, I can coax three orgasms out of her, and the third might be the hardest to get, but it's also the most rewarding for both of us.

Our rhythm speeds up, and I feel her body responding. I change the angle slightly, lifting one of her legs up, allowing me to grind my pelvis against her clit with each thrust. She starts to tighten around me and I keep thrusting, making sure to hit that magical spot as she rides the waves of her orgasm.

I bring my lips back to her and kiss her leisurely as I slow my thrusts down. I'm holding back my own release, wanting to coax that third orgasm from her, if I can.

Once I feel Lauren completely relax and go into that languid state of bliss, I stop my thrusts completely and rest my forehead against the crook of her neck.

I drop a few kisses against the skin there, tasting the saltiness of her skin and the thin sheen of sweat that has started to gather. Once she's recovered from the orgasm, I flip us over so she's on top of me. She quickly sinks back down on my cock and the angle in which she sits makes me feel like I'm so fucking deep inside her, my eyes nearly roll back in my head.

I let her take control, aiding her body as she lifts and drops. I reach up and cup her breasts, rolling her nipples between my fingers, before I sit up enough to take one into my mouth, sucking and flicking it with my tongue.

"That's it, baby, take what you need," I tell her as I feel her chasing that third elusive orgasm.

I hold on to her hips, thrusting up a few times to meet her own downward thrusts, then slip a hand between us and rub her clit with the pad of my thumb.

"S-S-S-Sam. Oh! D-D-don't stop!" She cries out as I increase the pressure, the speed, and drive of my thrusts. I know the moment her orgasm hits her as she completely falls apart in my arms. It quickly sends me over the edge and I bask in the bliss of it all. She's absolutely stunning when she falls apart like this, and I just hold on tight as her body milks my own of every last drop of my release.

Lauren collapses forward on my body as we both share in a blissed-out state. I slowly stroke her back, feeling her relax even further into me. I can feel myself starting to slip from her body as my erection softens inside her.

"Ren, baby. I need to take care of the condom," I say against her skin as I start to roll us to the side. She's in such a state of bliss, she almost looks like she's asleep. I slip away from her and into the bathroom to clean up. I quickly do my business and climb right back into bed with her, pulling her close, back into my arms.

We eventually settle, with me on my back and Lauren on her side, her head on my chest and leg draped over my own. I wrap my arm around her shoulders, my hand resting on her lower back and hip area. She draws lazy circles on my abdomen with her fingers, as she traces the lines of my muscles.

"I love you," she whispers into the darkened room.

"I love you, too, Ren," I reply, as sleep overtakes us.

24

LAUREN

WE LEISURELY WAKE UP THE NEXT DAY, AND AFTER A ROUND OF slow morning sex, we get moving, taking a joint shower then grabbing some breakfast. We pack an overnight bag and decide to head to the Outer Banks for the night. The drive is beautiful, and once we arrive at the beach, I'm so glad we decided to come. We check into our B&B that we found online and head out to explore.

We walk hand in hand along the beach, just taking in the scenery and enjoying being together. The complete easiness and comfort we have between us makes this moment almost perfect. Neither one of us feels the need to fill the silence with unneeded words.

"I put in for a transfer for an opening back home," Sam finally says, breaking that silence.

I stumble mid-step, causing him to grab my hips so I don't tumble over.

"What, when, why didn't you tell me?" I ask, a little shocked at his announcement.

"I just did it before you got here. The posting states it's for the large office in Louisville, but I talked to them to see if the job could be done from the smaller field office in Lexington. They didn't see why it couldn't, with the knowledge that I'd have to travel to the main office occasionally."

"So, does that mean you got the transfer and are moving back home?"

"Not yet. It can take a few weeks sometimes for transfers to be approved. Even if they approve it and I can't work from the field office, it would still put us a whole hell of a lot closer than we are right now, and that's all I care about. As much as this distance was probably a good thing over these past few weeks, I'm already over it. I want to see you every day, and not just through a video chat. Now that I've kissed you, and made love to you, I want that option every day. And I know you wouldn't want to move out here, so I didn't ever want to ask. Plus, I wouldn't mind moving back home. I miss being back there and around everyone all the time."

I come to a complete stop and turn so I'm facing him. Sam's arms naturally wrap around me, pulling me closer. I can't hide the smile on my face at his news, and I shock him slightly when I jump up, wrapping my legs around his body and my arms around his neck, and plant my lips against his.

"This is the best news," I say against his mouth.

He rests his forehead against mine and just smiles at me.

"I know you've been looking for a new place these past few weeks, but did you maybe want to expand that search and find something together once I know for sure the transfer is going to go through and where I'll be working out of?" he asks, the hopefulness evident in his voice. "No pressure, and I understand if you still need time to be on your own."

"I don't need anything but you," I tell him before I kiss him again.

WE RETURN FROM OUR IMPROMPTU TRIP TO THE BEACH THE next night. We enjoyed ourselves so much and made so many fun memories together. After Sam told me about his pending transfer, I've been happier, and this weight I didn't even realize was hanging over me lifted. Knowing he wants to move home and make this work between the two of us makes me love him that much more. He wants to make me happy, and coming to me just goes to show how big of a heart he has.

With only one full day left before I have to go home, we call it an early evening after returning from the beach, only unpacking our overnight bags and starting a load of laundry before ordering in some dinner. We cuddle up on the couch after eating and watch a movie before we crawl into bed.

We cuddle up with each other after making love slowly. Not in any rush to finish, nor making it about the chase of the orgasms. This was pure love-making; a soul-connecting, earth-shattering connection between two individuals who love each other more than words can ever describe.

"I was thinking we could go out for another hike tomorrow morning, and then go walk around at some of the touristy shops in the afternoon if you'd like. Dave also texted, asking if we wanted to get together again for dinner. He said Meg wanted to see you again before you leave on Tuesday morning."

"That sounds like a good day to me. Maybe before dinner, we can come back here so I can get most of my things packed back up. That way I'm not rushed if dinner runs late."

"We can definitely do that."

"Did you want to invite them over here instead?" I ask.

"We can, or we can go out. What would you prefer?"

"Let's have them over, that way we don't feel rushed by a restaurant if we want to leisurely eat and visit like we did the other night. You can grill, or I can make something. If I'm going to cook something big, we might need to cut our afternoon shopping short, but otherwise, I think we'll be fine."

"Whatever you want to do is fine with me," Sam says, kissing the top of my head.

"Let's grill. I can make a salad and a side, and you can make steaks."

"Sounds good, babe. I'll text Dave in the morning and let him know," Sam says, squeezing me tight before we both drift off to sleep.

I'M IN THE KITCHEN, FINISHING UP THE PASTA SALAD WHEN I hear two knocks on the front door, and then it opens.

"We're here, put your clothes back on!" Dave hollers out as he and Meg walk inside. I laugh, remembering Sam saying almost the exact same thing when we walked into their house the other night.

"I'm in the kitchen," I call out. "Come on in."

"Good to see you, Lauren," Meg greets me when they walk into the kitchen.

"Good to see you guys again. How was your weekend?"

"It was good, really good," she says, looking up at her husband with a smile on her face. I can see the love they have for each other rolling off of them in waves. Knowing the heartache they've been through breaks my heart, but I'm glad they came out the other side of it stronger and more in love with each other than before. He bends down and places a kiss on her lips before stepping away, out onto the patio where Sam has already started the steaks.

"How long have the two of you been married?" I ask, realizing it never came up the other night.

"We just celebrated our tenth wedding anniversary in May, but we've been together for about fifteen years. We met in college and have been inseparable ever since. Well, I take that back. We became inseparable once we started dating. That happened a few months after he broke up with one of my roommates." She laughs and looks toward the patio door to where her husband stands, talking to Sam.

"Congratulations!"

"Thanks. It's been a good ten years, for the most part. We've had our trials, some really low lows, but also some really high highs. We've learned a lot about ourselves, individually and as a couple, and I wouldn't want to do life with anyone else."

"I'm so glad you have each other. Sam told me what happened, and I'm so sorry you guys went through all of that."

"Thank you, we miss him every day. I stop and think what kind of little boy he'd be like often. What it would be like to have a toddler running around ruling our lives. Whenever I see a little boy about his age, I smile and picture him doing the same things. It took me a long time to cope and not break down anytime I was around kids, especially ones his age, but I've gotten much better with it in the past year or so. Just took time to grieve and heal."

"I'm glad to hear that you've found a way to do that," I comment, as the door opens and the guys step inside.

"The steaks are done, did you ladies want to eat outside?" Sam asks.

"Sure, let me just grab everything and we can head out."

"Can we grab anything for you?" Sam offers.

"Yes please, here's the salad and pasta salad." I hand over the bowls. "Dave, if you can grab everyone's drinks, I can grab the dishes."

We make our way outside, all taking a seat around the table and digging into the food. We chat about our trip to the beach and what else we've done while I've been in town. We finish up dinner, and relax around the table, enjoying each other's company.

"Well, we have some news," Meg says, looking over at Dave with a small smile on her face. I notice the shift in both of them and they silently communicate whatever it is they are about to tell me and Sam.

"We're pregnant," she finally says, a shaky smile filling her face. I immediately look at Dave to see a similar expression on his face.

"That's amazing news! Congratulations!" I almost yell.

"I'm so happy for you both," Sam adds. "When are you due?"

"I'm just about thirteen weeks now, so I'm due around mid-February. So far, everything looks good." Meg pauses and looks over at Dave, a huge smile on both of their faces. He reaches over and rubs her belly before clasping her hand in his own.

"My doctor is going to watch things closely toward the end, and has warned me already that I need to be prepared for either an induction or scheduled C-section as early as thirty-seven weeks, if they feel I need the baby to come a little bit early," Meg explains, dropping her other hand to her itty-bitty baby bump that I can totally see, now that she's announced the pregnancy.

"Will you find out the sex?" I ask, not knowing if they found out before.

"Oh yes! I'm a planner and need to know," Meg replies, and the guys just laugh.

"When do you get to find out?"

"Usually around twenty weeks. My next appointment is when I'm sixteen weeks, and I'll be able to schedule the big ultrasound when I'm at that appointment."

"That's so exciting! You'll have to let me know once you find out!" I tell her excitedly.

Our conversation stays light and cheerful after the baby news. I can't believe how giddy I am for them. After knowing everything they've been through, this baby will be such a blessing to them. I'm just sad to know that we—well, at least, I—won't be around to see the baby grow up. I feel like I've been friends with Dave and Meg for years, not just a few days. I don't know if it's the bond that Sam has with them or just how quickly they accepted me into their little group, but I'm really going to miss them when I head back home, and Sam hopefully follows me not much longer after that.

25

SAM

LAUREN IS QUIET AFTER DAVE AND MEG LEAVE, THE REALITY that she's leaving in the morning setting in. We've had such an amazing week together, and I don't want it to end. I'm hopeful that my transfer will go through quickly, and we can be together all the time in just a few weeks, maybe two months, at most.

"I'm so happy for them," she finally says, breaking the silence.

"Me too. I can tell they are trying to stay as positive as possible, but when you've lived through what they have, it's hard not to think about all the 'what-ifs' the entire time."

"I can't even imagine what it must be like for them. But I just know they'll both be great parents."

"That they will be. They'd planned for Meg to stop working back when Jack was born, but with the stillbirth, she ended up going back to work after awhile off. I think she needed something to fill her time and mind. So, I'm sure they're considering the same thing this time, as well."

"We'll have to plan a trip back here for after the baby's

born, to see them. I'm choosing to think positive, that your transfer will get approved."

"I think that's a great idea," I tell her. "Would you like something else to drink?"

"A glass of wine would be perfect," she answers as she gets up from the couch. "I'm going to go finish up the little bit of packing I have left to do before morning."

After grabbing our drinks, I follow her into the bedroom and hand her the glass of wine before I sit down on the bed, watching her.

"Need any help?" I offer after a few minutes.

"I think I'm good, just making sure everything's going to fit correctly. I'll still need to put in my bathroom stuff in the morning."

"When you're done, I was thinking we could go curl up together on the couch and watch a movie, or some TV if you prefer," I tell her as she zips up the suitcase and moves it to sit along the wall on her side of the bed.

"I was thinking we could cuddle in bed." She winks at me.

"That will work, too," I toss right back at her as I pat the bed next to me.

She climbs on the bed and leans against me as I sit up against the headboard.

"Is this what you had in mind?" I ask, leaning my head against hers.

"Not exactly." She turns her head, knocking mine off of hers so she can look up at me, the heavy look of desire written all over her face.

I drop my lips to hers for a moment, not giving her the deep kiss she's searching for. "What is it you had in mind?" I ask against her lips.

"Less clothes, more skin." She nips at my bottom lip.

I roll us over so she's lying flat on the bed and I'm positioned over her. I've got all my weight pushed up and off of her, hovering a full arm's length from her body.

"You're beautiful, you know that?" I tell her, hoping she believes that completely. I'm not expecting an answer, as it was more of a rhetorical question. I take my time scanning her body with my eyes. I want nothing more than to strip her down and fuck her until she can't walk the next day. But I also want to take care of her and cherish her, protecting her against everything in life.

"Can you kiss me now?" she asks finally.

I drop my body weight down onto my forearms and bring one hand up to cup her cheek, staring into her eyes for a few moments before I give her what she's asked for. It starts out light and easy, and slowly morphs into something deeper, something more.

We don't rush anything. I think we're both trying to savor this, since it's our last night together until either one of us goes to visit the other or I get my transfer and move back home for good.

It takes awhile before we start stripping each other out of our clothes, but once we do finally get each other naked, I quickly grab a condom from the bedside table and roll it down my cock. I line myself up with her pussy and thrust my way in, not stopping until I'm deeply seated inside of her. A few cries of pleasure ring from her lips as I still inside her.

I start rocking in-out-in-out at a slow pace. I bring my lips back to hers and claim her mouth with my own. No rush to the end; I want to savor every second of this night. Make it last until the next time we see each other, however long that might be.

I WAKE UP BEFORE LAUREN THE NEXT MORNING, WRAPPED around her naked body. I've only had her in my bed and arms for the past week, but I've already grown to expect her there. I'm going to really miss having her here, in my everyday life and bed each night.

I stay as still as I can, just memorizing the feel of her against me. What her skin and hair smells like against my own. The pull to wake her up so we can have one last time to make love, to last us for the next few weeks or possibly months, is strong. I'd gone into last night thinking it was going to be the last time, but I just can't stop myself from kissing along her exposed neck until she's stirring awake in my arms, turning to face me.

"Good morning, beautiful," I whisper against her lips.

"Good morning," she murmurs before I slant my lips over hers and kiss her hard.

I roll her under me and slip inside her, swallowing her moans as I kiss her. I start out slowly as we both wake up. Lazy morning sex—who knew it could be so amazing.

"Damn, baby, you feel so good," I grit out, as I start to increase my thrusts. I push up and then drop my head down to suck a nipple into my mouth.

I sit back slightly on my knees, watching as I drive in and out of Lauren, then come to a stop.

"Fuck!" I yell.

"Wh-what's wrong?" Lauren sits up abruptly.

"I forgot a fucking condom. No wonder it felt so different, so fucking good. I'm so sorry, Lauren."

"Sam."

"Shit, I didn't—"

"*Sam!*" she yells, to get my attention.

I look up at her, feeling so guilty for forgetting. I know she can't be on birth control and as much as I look forward to babies with Lauren in the future, now is not that time.

"It's okay, Sam. Don't beat yourself up about it. I got wrapped up in the moment just as much as you did. Put one on now and we can move forward. If, for some reason, anything was to come from it, we'll deal with it. We love each other and while a baby now would be a little sooner than I think either of us planned, it wouldn't be the end of the world either," she states as she reaches over and grabs a condom from the nightstand and hands it to me.

I take a deep breath and quickly put it on, then get back to making love to this woman, thinking the entire time, how in the hell did I get so lucky to have her in my life and to have her love.

26

LAUREN

"Ready?" Sam asks me after we finish our quick breakfast. I need to be to the airport for my flight in about thirty minutes and after his sexy wake up this morning, we spent a little longer in bed and the shower than I'd planned. So, a quick breakfast it was. Thankfully, I'd pretty much packed everything last night, only needing to toss in my bathroom things, and my chargers and such.

"As ready as I can be," I answer somberly.

"Don't be sad, baby. We'll see each other again soon," he tells me, trying to cheer me up. "And in the meantime, we've got technology to keep us in touch." He winks at me.

"I know, I'm just going to miss you. Miss kissing you and the feel of your arms around me each night. I'm going to sleep like shit the next few nights, missing you next to me in bed."

"Me too, babe, me too."

Sam loads my bag into his truck and I bring out my carry-on bag. I've got my kindle all charged and ready to go to help me drown out my sadness of leaving Sam behind, not knowing for sure when I'll see him again.

We drive, hand in hand, all the way to the airport in silence. Neither one of us is ready for this trip to be over. I'm so glad that I came and that we made these strides in our relationship, solidifying what we are and how we feel about each other in this aspect. The physical connection we found together is like none other, and it makes me excited to see where we can take things as our relationship progresses.

Sam pulls into the short-term parking garage and quickly finds a spot. We silently climb out of the truck, him grabbing my suitcase and me grabbing my carry-on bag. I sling it over my shoulder and come around the front of his truck, slipping my hand into his as we walk toward the ticket counter level.

I make quick work of checking my bag and dropping it off. We slowly walk toward the security area, knowing we have to say goodbye on this side of it.

Sam pulls me off to the side, into a little alcove that gives us a bit of privacy. He cups my face in his hands and brings his forehead down to mine.

"I'm going to miss you so damn much, Ren," he says, placing a kiss against my forehead. The intimacy of that kiss has me falling deeper in love with him.

"Ditto," is all I can tell him without the sadness taking over and the tears spilling out. I take a few breaths, calming myself before I attempt to speak. "When do you think you'll hear about the transfer?"

"Hopefully by the end of this week, if everything goes to plan, but sometimes these things can take forever. But as soon as I know, you'll be my first call."

I look down at my watch and more time has slipped by than I thought. "Shit, I've got to get going. I don't want to miss my flight. Well, I wouldn't mind staying here with you a few more days, but you know what I mean," I ramble on.

"Babe," he says, stopping me, and then kissing me. "You'll be fine. Now promise you'll text me once you board and then once you land. I'll call you tonight once I'm home from work, as well."

"Okay." I give him a shaky smile before I lean up to kiss him again.

"I should go," I say as I break the kiss, pulling him in for a tight hug.

"I love you," he whispers against my neck.

"Love you, too," I reply as we break apart and step out of the alcove. He keeps hold of my hand until we reach the end of the security line, pulling me back in for one last hug and kiss.

"I love you," he whispers against my lips again, and I giggle.

"I know, you just told me that a few seconds ago."

"I know, I just needed to say it again. Make sure you don't forget," he says before I step away from him, breaking our full body contact.

I take a few steps down the roped-off security line, thankful it's pretty empty. I look over my shoulder to him, blowing him a kiss, and mouthing, "I love you" to him. He smiles at my gesture and watches as I reach the front of the security line and through the checkpoint. As soon as I'm through, I walk over to the hall I'd be able to exit from to wave, and blow him one last kiss before I force myself to head for my gate.

Thankfully, my flight home is pretty uneventful. I text Sam right away, letting him know I made it safely. Now, to just wait for him to call me once he's home tonight. He wasn't sure if he'd be slammed at work or not, after taking off the past few days with me in town.

I make it home and get my things unpacked and laundry

going right away. I've got another week before I need to get my classroom set up for the school year, so I plan to enjoy the remainder of my summer break.

"Hey!" Mom greets me as she comes in from the garage, setting down the bags of groceries in her hands. "How was your trip?"

"It was great! Do you have more bags to come in?" I ask.

"Yep, just another load," she says as she walks back out to the garage. I step out with her and grab a few of the bags, then shut her trunk once she's got everything out.

"So, tell me all about it. How was Sam?"

I think for a few moments, not quite sure how to put into words how amazing the past week was.

"He's great. We're great," I tell her, blushing a little. My mom and I have always had a great relationship, but discussing my sex life with her has never been our thing. I'm sure she knows it's part of my life, but it's not like we're over here drinking wine and discussing our favorite positions.

"What did you guys do?"

"We went on a few hikes and oh my, was it beautiful. I got to meet some of his friends and see where he works. We went down to the Outer Banks for one night, and spent almost two full days down there enjoying the beach. His friends, Dave and Meg, were super nice. I felt like I'd known them my whole life after just one visit. We had dinner together twice, and at the second dinner, they told us they're expecting." I go on to tell my mom a little bit of their story as I help her put away the groceries.

"Meg and I have started to text each other. I love having a new friend, but it just sucks she lives so far away."

"I'm glad you had such a good time."

"Me too, Mom. It was exactly what we needed to make our relationship stronger, and to see if we could actually make this work. Oh, and the best news to come out of my trip was Sam telling me that he's put in for a transfer to the local office! They've had a position open for a while now, and not only is he confident that he'll get it, but that they'll allow him to work primarily out of the local office and only have to go into the big office for meetings or special occasions."

"That'd be fantastic. I'm sure his parents would be ecstatic if he moved back home."

"I think so. He's not mentioning it to many people yet until he hears a definitive answer, so keep that to yourself, please."

"Your, or should I say *his*, secret is safe with me."

"So, with him possibly moving here, we were thinking of getting a place together if he does get transferred. So, my plan for now is to hold off on looking any more at places until he knows for sure. Because there's always the possibility he'll get transferred, but have to work full-time out of the main office. If that's the case, then we'd probably look for something that's a little more centrally-located between his work and my school."

"That's probably a good idea to wait then."

"So, you and Dad are still okay with me crashing here until we know more?" I ask.

"Of course, sweetheart. You know you're always welcome here at home, and for as long as you need," she assures me.

"Thanks," I say, handing her the last of the refrigerator items.

"Do you have any plans tonight?" she asks as she moves on from putting groceries away to making dinner.

"Nope, just planned to hang out here at home and have a quiet evening. I've already got my laundry going, and now I'm just waiting for Sam to call once he's home from work."

"Ah, well, dinner will be ready in about an hour or so. Once I've got it started, I was going to sit out on the deck and drink a glass of wine while I read another couple chapters in my new book."

I got my love of reading from my mother. She's always been one to have a book in her hand, or at least within reach. When ebooks became an option, I swear her reading went through the roof, as it was so accessible for her.

"Sounds like a good plan. I might join you, so I can get a little further in the book I've been reading the past few days."

I leave the kitchen when I hear the chime from the washer letting me know it's finished with the load. I quickly transfer the clothes to the dryer before I take the few items into my room that need to be hung up to air dry. The sound of my phone alerting me to a new text has me reaching for my phone.

Sam: Hey babe. Glad you made it home safely. I've been slammed since I walked in the doors this morning. We started a huge new case that's requiring all hands on deck, and is going to take us a bit. I'll call you when I get home, I just don't know when that will be yet. If you haven't heard from me yet and you're ready to go to bed, just shoot me a text so that I don't accidentally wake you up if I was to call.

I read Sam's text over quickly, feeling bad for him that he's just now getting to take his first very short break to text me.

Lauren: Hey, sorry you're so slammed. I hope you get to go

home at a decent time. I miss you already and am going to miss you wrapped around me tonight. Love you. XOXO

I busy myself with hanging up the items I brought into my room and then dig out my kindle. I stop in the kitchen long enough to grab a glass of lemonade, then head out to the deck to lie in a lounge chair and read until dinner is ready.

A little while later, I'm pulled from my book with a new text alert.

Zoey: Hey girlie, did you make it back?
Lauren: Yep, got in this afternoon. It was an amazing trip! Can't wait to see you and tell you all about it. When are you free this week?
Zoey: We could get together Thursday night for dinner and drinks if that works for you? Either go out or you could come over here? If you come here, bring an overnight bag and then you can just crash here, and we can drink copious amounts of wine and dish all night!
Lauren: Sounds like a date. 😊

27

SAM

It's midnight before I make it out of the office, tired as hell after the busy day I had. We made great headway in cracking the case and tracking down the criminals we were after. I'm ready for something to eat, and my bed, which is going to feel empty without Lauren in it tonight. I got so used to having her in it with me over the last week. I can only hope my transfer comes through soon, or else I'm going to go crazy without her, now that we've solidified our relationship and taken it to that next level.

I pull my cell phone out of my pocket, once I'm inside and sitting down to eat the fast food I picked up on my way home. I see a couple texts from Lauren and immediately a smile breaks out on my lips. The first one was a reply to my quick text to her this afternoon. I was so busy after that few moments I texted her earlier that I never noticed her reply, as well as a second one only about a half hour ago, telling me she was headed to bed.

Sam: Hey, I just got home. Are you still awake? If you aren't, I love you and call me in the morning. I won't be

**going into the office until late morning. If you're still
awake, call or FaceTime me.**

Figuring she's already asleep, I pull up Facebook and
start scrolling through my feed, catching up on what my
friends and family are up to.

I'm just about finished with my food when Lauren's face
fills my screen, attempting to FaceTime with me.

"Hey, beautiful," I greet her, as soon as our video
connects. She's sitting up on her bed, covers pulled up
around her. There's not a stitch of makeup on her face, and
her hair is piled on the top of her head in a messy bun. She's
looks just as beautiful now as she does all made up and
ready to go out. My heart clenches that she's so far away
from me and I can't reach out and touch her, or better yet,
crawl into bed and hold her in my arms.

"Hey. How're you doing?" she asks, a small yawn
escaping her lips.

"Better now," I tell her, smiling at her through the
camera. "I figured I'd missed you and you'd already be
asleep."

"I was reading and was just about to go to sleep for the
night, but when I saw your text, I couldn't go to bed without
seeing you, for a few minutes at least," she says, smiling
at me.

"I'm glad you called. Did you have a good evening?"

"Yep, got all my laundry done, read some, visited with
Mom and Dad a bit. They're fine with me staying here as
long as needed until you know for sure about your transfer
and we can find a place together."

"That's good. Hopefully I'll hear soon about the transfer.
But with this case we're working on, I might not hear much
until it's finalized. The field agents were able to catch the

guys, but we still have to finish collecting and analyzing some of the evidence, which can take weeks, if any lab reports are needed. We were just lucky to catch these guys so fast," I tell her, scrubbing my face with a hand. The fatigue is starting to set in, now that I'm not focusing on tracking down the money these guys were laundering through multiple accounts.

"You look about as exhausted as I feel. Why don't I let you go and we can talk tomorrow when we're both not about to fall asleep on camera," she suggests, giggling a little.

"Sounds good, babe. With how late I was at the office tonight, I'm not going in until late morning, unless they call me earlier. So call me when you're up."

"Okay, will do. Love you," she says, blowing me a kiss.

"G'night, beautiful. I love you. Dream of me holding you."

"Always," she says, before the connection cuts out between us. I get up and toss out the trash from my food, then head for my bathroom to get ready for bed.

Once in my bed, I sink beneath the cover and the smell from Lauren on my sheets surrounds me. Her lavender shampoo and body wash linger in the air and make me ache for her that much more. I grab the pillow she used, holding it against my chest and breathing deeply, pulling her smell further into my lungs as I drift off to sleep, wishing like hell that I was hugging her and not just the pillow she used.

THE WEEK PASSES BY ABOUT THE SAME. I WORK CRAZY HOURS on this current case and only get stolen moments to text and chat with Lauren. I still haven't heard any news on my transfer request, but I'm still hopeful that it should come through, and hopefully soon.

We wrapped up our case today, so I'll be getting out of the office at a decent time, thankfully. With all the hours I've put in the past week, I've earned some comp time, and decided to surprise Lauren by flying in late tonight and staying for the next few days. School starts the middle of next week, so she'll be busy some of the time, getting her classroom set up and teacher meetings, but I just miss her so damn much. So, one day while she's in meetings, I'm going to drive up to the main field office and see if I can talk with the deputy in charge and get my transfer moving.

I'm on my way out of the office when I hear my name being called from down the hall.

"Sam!" I turn around and see Dave standing outside his office, waving me over.

"What's up?"

"Not much, just about to head out myself. What are you doing tonight? Want to come over and have dinner with Meg and me?"

"Not tonight. I'm headed home to throw together a bag, and flying home to surprise Ren for the next couple of days."

"Ah, have a good time then. I'll see you when you get back," he says, a shit-eating grin on his face. He slaps my back as we both walk out of his office.

Dave and I have just stepped out into the waiting area, when Becky pops her head up from behind her desk.

"Sam," she calls before Dave and I can get onto the elevator.

"Yes, Miss Becky?"

"How's that nice young lady doing?"

"She's great," I tell her, chuckling to myself. "I'm actually getting ready to fly out to surprise her for the next few days. Now that we've closed out the case and I have some time I can take off, I figured why not go and see her."

"Well, before you go and have a great time with her, the boss man wants to see you." She nods her head toward his office.

"Thanks, Becky. I'll go see him now. I'll see you next week sometime."

"Have a great time," she says as I turn to head back toward the office.

"I'll catch you later!" I holler at Dave, who waited around while I talked to Becky.

"Have a good time with Lauren. When you get back, we'll get together for that dinner," he says before the doors close to the elevator.

"Agent Wentz," I greet as I walk through the open door of my boss's office. He's the Special Agent in Charge of this office.

"Sam." He stands, offering his hand for me to shake. He's about fifteen or so years older than me, and has been with the FBI since he was in his early twenties. "Close the door and take a seat."

I do as he asks, quickly sitting in the chair across from his desk. He removes his glasses, setting them on the desk in front of him.

"Your transfer has been processed and granted. They'd like for you to start in the new office in the next three to four weeks, if possible. So, whatever works best for you is fine with me."

I'm sure the smile on my face is giving away how excited I am that this has come through! Now, I'm even more excited to surprise Lauren tonight. Maybe while I'm in town, we can go and look at some places to possibly rent and get that ball rolling.

"Thank you so much, sir. I can't tell you how much I was looking forward to getting news about this transfer. I've really enjoyed my time here, but it's time I go back home. I've got some important people waiting for me there."

"We'll miss you around here. You're a good agent, Sam. A real asset to the agency. Keep doing what you're good at and you'll go far."

"Thank you," I sincerely state, standing and accepting his outstretched hand to shake again.

"Enjoy your next couple of days off. You won't have much time left here in this office once you're back, so we'll need to make sure nothing is outstanding on any of the cases you've worked on in the past six or so months, and then we can get you cleared out. Give you some time to get moved before you need to start at the new office. Now get out of here," he says with a smile.

I leave his office, not quite sure how I'm going to keep myself from calling Lauren to tell her the news. I'm already about to burst from the happiness that we'll be together soon.

I practically sprint out of the office, headed for the stairs, not wanting to wait for the elevator.

"We'll miss you, Sam," I hear Becky call out to me as I sprint past her desk, bringing me to a skidding halt, and I grin. *Of course she already knows. She knows everything around here.*

"Thanks, Becky. I'll miss you all, too. It's just time. That, and Lauren is my home, and I need to be where she is."

"Oh, I understand completely. Go get your girl," she says, coming around her desk to wrap me in a hug. Becky is like a second mom to me, hell, to this entire department. I've spent plenty of Thanksgivings and Fourth of July's at her home. She tends to make sure all the single agents have a place to go for the important holidays, if they aren't returning home to see family.

"See you next week," I tell her once she releases me from the hug, and I dash for the stairs again.

I jump in my truck, headed for home as quickly as I can.

"Hey," Steven greets as he answers his cell. "Haven't talked to you in forever. What's up, man?"

"Sorry, been swamped with a case. But we finalized everything on it today. I need your help with something," I tell him as I continue to drive.

"What's that?"

"I'm flying in late tonight to surprise Lauren. I land around 11:15, so I should be able to get to your place by midnight. Anyway, can you convince her to come over and hang out, and I'll surprise her there?"

"Sure, I'll see if she can babysit. Renee has been wanting to go out, and we just haven't made plans happen yet. I'm sure Lauren would be up to playing with Ethan for a few hours tonight."

"Thanks, man. I owe you one," I tell him, my plans hopefully falling into place. "How's life with a one-year-old treating you?"

"Great. He's growing so fast. You won't believe it when you see him again. He's so close to walking on his own. I bet by next week, he finds the confidence to let go and do it on his own. Renee has been working with him, trying to get him to do it for a week now, and he's just so close."

"That's awesome, man." I almost slip up and say something to the effect that I won't have to miss much more of his life now that I'm moving home. But I want Lauren to be the first person I tell that news to.

We shoot the shit for a few more minutes as I finish my drive. Steven promises me he'll get Lauren over to his house and figure out a way to keep her there until I can arrive. I then plan to whisk her away to the hotel I still need to book once I make it home.

28

LAUREN

Steven: Hey sis, any chance you can watch Ethan tonight, so I can take Renee out to dinner, maybe a movie?
Lauren: An evening with my sweet nephew? Of course! What time do you want me to come over?
Steven: By 5? Renee doesn't know yet, so anytime before then. I need to figure out where to take her and see if there's any good movies playing that we can catch.
Lauren: Sounds good, I'll finish up what I'm working on and head over. Do you have anything I can make him and I for dinner, or should I just plan on ordering in something after the two of you leave?
Steven: I'm sure Renee has something you can have, otherwise order what you want and it's my treat for helping me out on such short notice.
Lauren: Aww such a sweet older brother I have. I'll see you soon!

WITH NEW EVENING PLANS NOW IN PLACE, I FINISH UP MAKING desk nameplates for my students. Thankfully, I only have two left to do. These always take me awhile to make because I inevitably mess up on more than one and am such a perfectionist that I will do them over until they're perfect.

I clean up the supplies I was using and lock up my classroom before heading over to Renee and Steven's house. They don't live too far away from our parents' house, so my drive isn't very long. On my way over, I think of what's almost always on my mind—Sam.

As I pull into their driveway, my phone dings, alerting me to a new text message. Once I'm parked and have my car turned off, I pull my cell out and see my man's name on the screen.

Sam: Hey Beautiful. Busy day here again today. I probably won't be home until late, can you stay up, so we can FaceTime?

Lauren: Hi! I just got to Steven & Renee's to babysit for the evening, so I'm sure I'll be up late. FT me when you get home. Even if I'm sleeping, I'll wake up to see your handsome face. 🙂

Sam: Sounds good babe. I've got to get back to the bullpen, but I love you and I'll talk to you later.

Lauren: I love you too!

I toss my phone back in my purse and head into the house.

"Hey! I'm here! Where's my favorite nephew?" I call out as I walk toward the living room, where I can hear baby giggles and some kid's show playing on the TV.

"Hi!" Renee says to me once I enter the room. "What a surprise! Is everything all right?" she asks from the floor where she's obviously been playing with Ethan.

"Oh, Steven texted me earlier, asking if I would come watch Little Man, so you guys could go out. I guess he forgot to tell you," I tell her, laughing at my brother's stupidity of not informing his wife of these plans. "Crap, I hope I didn't just ruin any surprise he might have had planned. But he knew I was headed over here soon, so I'm surprised he hasn't told you yet. Maybe he got busy at work and didn't have time to text you?"

Before she can reply, her phone starts buzzing on the floor next to her.

"Speaking of the devil," she says, answering her phone. "Hey, babe. Yep, she just got here a couple minutes ago." She pauses as he talks to her. "Okay, sounds good. I'll go take a quick shower and see you soon." Another short pause on her end. "Love you, too," she says before hanging up.

"I guess I need to go shower and get ready. Thanks for coming over tonight to hang out with this little man." Renee stands up and heads for the stairs.

"Ethan, come to Auntie," I say to my nephew, getting down onto the floor and holding out one of his toys to grab his attention. He plops down and crawls over to me, peppering my face with open-mouthed baby kisses. I just love this little boy so much and can't wait until I'm a mom. That dream doesn't feel like such a far-off possibility with Sam in my life now. I know it's still at least a year or two away, but it still feels within reach.

Ethan and I have a fun time playing while Renee is busy getting ready. While she's still upstairs doing her thing, Steven gets home. The squeals and Ethan's "Da da" when he hears him come in just melts my heart all over again.

"Hey, Little Man. Were you good for Momma today?" he asks his son as he picks him up, getting the same slobbery kisses as I did.

"Ma ma ma..." Ethan babbles after attacking Steven's face.

"You be good for Auntie Ren tonight." He kisses his son's head. "Thanks again for doing this for us tonight," he says, setting Ethan back down on the floor amongst the toys.

"Anytime. I really don't mind."

"I'm going to go change quick and see if Renee is close to being ready to go. Did you ask her about food for the two of you?"

"No, I didn't get the chance to before she went to shower."

"I'll ask her and let you know, or you can just go see what we've got."

"I'm a big girl, I can figure it out," I tell him, laughing as I shoo him out of the room.

"Come on, Ethan, let's go see what Auntie Ren can find for us to eat." I swing him up into my arms and blow a raspberry against his neck. The giggles that fall from his lips are so cute and make me continue to attack his neck with more kisses and raspberries.

After finding something for Ethan to eat, I pull out my cell and place a delivery order for myself. I'd been in a Chinese mood all day and had planned on ordering anyway, so it doesn't make any difference to me if I eat it here versus at home with Mom and Dad.

Ethan chows down on the food I placed before him on his highchair tray. He's getting so big! I can't believe he turned one a few weeks ago!

"En! En!" He bangs his sippy cup against his tray.

"Say that again!" I tell him, thinking he just tried to say my name. The excitement over that brings a huge smile to my face.

"En, En!" he says again, smiling at me.

"Look at you! Say Auntie Ren!"

"En!" he says one last time, and I just about choke on the emotion that's filling me.

"That's right, baby boy! You're so smart! Auntie Ren loves you!" I tell him, picking up his sippy cup for him again.

"He's playing a game with you," Renee says, walking into the kitchen as I'm picking up the cup. "He's figured out that if he drops stuff, it will get a reaction from the adults, so we've been not picking up the sippy super fast, trying to break him of the habit."

"Oh, sorry."

"Not your fault. Just thought I'd keep you from playing 'how many times can I make them pick up the sippy cup during one meal' game," she says, laughing.

"En! En!" Ethan calls out, hitting the tray for emphasis to get our attention.

"Did he just say what I think he said?" Renee asked, a little shocked.

"I think so!" I beam. "He's done it a few times since I put him in the chair to feed him."

"Aw, Ethan. You love Auntie Ren, don't you, sweet boy?"

"En! En!" he screeches, hitting his tray again, causing both of us to laugh at his antics.

He quiets down when I put a few more bites of food on his tray for him to feed himself.

"Did you find anything to eat? I'd kinda planned to order in takeout tonight. I never want to cook on Friday nights, so I'm sorry I didn't have anything easy for you to prepare."

"Oh, I'm good. I put in for a Chinese delivery order a few minutes ago. It should be here in the next half hour or so. Where are you two headed?"

"Steven was able to get us reservations for the Japanese

Steakhouse and then some tickets to the comedy club downtown. You don't mind being here that late, do you?"

"Not at all. If I get that tired, I can always crash in the guest room. Go, have fun. Don't worry one bit about Ethan or me. We'll both be just fine. Still his normal bedtime routine?"

"Yep, same as usual. He's really been enjoying his bath time lately, so feel free to stick him in early if he's fussy at all, or you want him to crash a little early. He's still working on getting in a few of his molars, so his sleeping has been so-so the last week or so. You can give him a dose of the Motrin that I have in the bin by his changing table if you'd like to help him fall asleep without the pain."

"Sure, I can make sure he gets that. Anything else?"

"Not that I can think of."

"Ready to go, babe?" my brother calls out to Renee as he steps in the room. It's almost sickening how cute they are together and how happy they both look.

"Yep, let me just give Ethan a kiss and hug goodbye, and then we can go," she tells him as she pulls Ethan out of the highchair.

"Thanks again, Ren. It will probably be eleven thirty, maybe eleven forty-five, before we're home."

"Don't worry. As I told Renee, Ethan and I will be perfectly fine. You guys go and have a great time."

"See ya!" they both call out after they've hugged and kissed Ethan goodbye, and then head toward the garage door.

I pick Ethan up after he's finished his dinner, and wash him off from the mess he's made with all his food. We play in the living room until my food is delivered and I make a small plate of food for me to eat quickly as he busies himself with his toys. I sit quietly, watching him while I eat. I can tell he's getting slightly tired by the way he's been rubbing his eyes the past couple of minutes, so as soon as I'm done eating, I take him upstairs for his bath and to get ready for bed.

The house is finally quiet, and I head for the living room. I quickly pick up all the toys so that Renee and Steven don't have to do it later tonight or in the morning. I grab a little more of my food, the baby monitor, and the TV remote, and plop myself down on the couch. I start flipping through the channels, trying to find something to watch for the next few hours.

I finally settled on a marathon of cooking shows on Food Network to pass the time. I've always enjoyed cooking, just never been too adventurous in the kitchen. I think it'd be fun to try some cooking classes sometime to learn some new skills to use in the kitchen.

I must have dozed off on the couch because I'm woken up by Renee and my brother coming in from the garage.

"Hi," Renee whispers. "Sorry to wake you."

"No, that's okay, I must have nodded off. How was dinner and the show?"

"It was great! My cheeks still hurt from laughing so hard. The comedians they had tonight were really good. Raunchy, but good."

I stand and stretch, waking myself up from my snooze on the couch.

"Did you want to stay here tonight?" Renee offers.

"No, I'm good. The drive home isn't that bad, and Sam was hopeful he'd be home to FaceTime me around midnight."

We sit and chat for a few more minutes, catching up with each other. I'm just about to stand to leave when I see a car pull into the driveway through the window. Guessing it's just someone using the driveway to turn around, I don't pay much attention to it and continue cleaning up my dishes and gathering my things to leave. When I walk back out to the living room, I'm floored when I see Sam standing just inside the door, a huge smile on his face.

29

SAM

"Hey." I greet Steven with a hug as I step inside. "Where is she?"

"Just stepped into the kitchen. I don't think she realized you pulled into the driveway."

Before I can move any further, Lauren comes back out and stands there, shocked to see me. The smile I had on my face widens as the stunned expression grows on Lauren's face.

"Sam! What are you doing here?" she almost yells as she runs and jumps into my arms, wrapping her legs around my waist and burying her face in my neck.

"I came to surprise you. We closed the case today, and with all the hours I put in over the last week, I earned a couple comp days, so I bought the first available ticket and came to see you."

"I can't believe you're here! Wait, how'd you know I was here and not at Mom and Dad's?" she questions, pulling back to look me in the eyes.

"Oh, I might have convinced Steven to get you over here

somehow. Looks like he came through for me. I didn't want to risk waking your parents with my late arrival."

"Where are you staying?" she asks, a slight blush creeping up her neck and onto her cheeks.

"I booked us a hotel," I answer before claiming her lips in a kiss.

"Get a room. That's my sister, man," Steven teases us, and I flip him the bird as I kiss Lauren harder.

We break apart, a whole hell of a lot sooner than I wanted to, but Lauren at least still has her brain functioning properly. I'm so lust-drunk and ready to get her to bed that it's practically all I can think about.

"Thanks for all your help tonight, but I think we're going to get out of here. You guys free tomorrow?" I ask Steven after I set Lauren down on her feet, placing a kiss against the top of her head once she's firmly back on the ground.

"We should be, you guys want to come over for dinner? We can grill and hang out on the deck. It's supposed to be nice out tomorrow," Renee offers.

"Sounds good to me." I look over at Lauren for her reaction.

"I'm fine with that," she says, smiling up at me. I can see the lust filling her eyes and know her mind is in the exact same place my own is.

We quickly say goodbye and make our exit.

"Do you want to follow me to the hotel, or leave your car here and we'll come get it in the morning?"

"We can just leave it here," she says as she walks up to the passenger side of my rental car.

I open the door for her and wait while she slips inside. I lean in and kiss her again, just a chaste one to hold me over until we make it to the hotel.

I quickly round the front of the car and get myself inside

and buckled up. "Did you want to stop by your parents' house to grab anything?"

"We can just go in the morning. I'm kinda getting tired, and it's so late already that I can just wait until then."

I reach over and lace my fingers with hers, bringing our joined hands to my mouth so I can kiss hers, then rest them on her leg for the remainder of the short ride over to the hotel.

"I can't believe you're here," she finally says, breaking the silence that filled the car.

"I missed you too much to just sit at home the next few days I have off. I needed to see you. Touch you. Taste and fuck you," I tell her, my voice dropping a bit on those last two sentiments. I notice a shiver go through her body from my words.

"Mmm. I'm glad you're here," she says, squeezing my hand a little harder.

We pull into the hotel and quickly exit the car. I grab my small suitcase from the back seat before coming around to grab Lauren's hand as we walk into the hotel. Checking in doesn't take long and we're soon in the elevator, on our way up to the third floor and to our room.

As soon as the door to our room is closed, I let go of my bag and wrap my arm around Lauren, pulling her flush against me and walking us over to the bed, my lips fused to hers.

Once we've hit the edge of the bed, I reach down and pick her up, laying her in the center of the bed. I hover over her, taking in my fill of her under me. The look of desire and love on her face has my blood pumping and wanting to sink inside her luscious body right this second. But that's not how tonight's going to go. I'm savoring every second that we have together.

"Are you just going to stare at me, or are you going to take off these clothes and put us both out of our misery?" she asks, a smirk covering that beautiful face of hers.

"I'll get there, I'm taking my time with you tonight. So, you just hold on to your patience tonight." I wink at her as I reach behind my head and pull my shirt off one-handed.

Her pupils dilate as her breathing hitches slightly, and I just smirk at her again. "See something you like?" I ask as I bring my mouth back to hers for a chaste kiss. I move my lips quickly from hers, across her cheek, down the angle of her jaw and the column of her neck. My couple-days-old beard scratching against her sensitive skin makes her squirm under me, driving me to continue my exploration of her body. I can feel her fingers as they graze along my skin, almost as if she's memorizing the dips of each of my muscles along my back and abdomen.

I take a little pity, nipping at her skin before I pull back. I need more access to her body, so I unbutton her shirt, then bring my lips back to her chest, dropping kisses along each patch of skin that's revealed as each button opens and exposes more to me. Once all the buttons are open and the shirt falls to the side, I unsnap her bra—*thank you whoever invented front-closure bras*—and quickly suck a hardened nipple into my mouth, rolling it with my tongue the way I know will drive her crazy.

"S-S-Sam!" Lauren cries out, arching up into me. I slide my hand over to cup her other breast and roll that nipple between my fingers. I eventually switch sides, lavishing the same attention with my mouth to the other side.

I eventually leave her breasts, kissing my way down her torso until I reach the waistband of her jeans, quickly unbuttoning them and sliding them down her hips, along with her panties. As I push them off, she sits up and fully removes her shirt and bra. I slide back up, capturing her lips with my own.

Deepening the kiss, she pushes me up and follows me as we both stand at the edge of the bed. I bring my hands up her body and feel hers as they slide to my waist, unbuckling my belt and then undoing the button and zipper. She slides her hands into the sides, effectively pushing my jeans and boxer briefs over my hips and to the floor. I step out of them, kicking them to the side. My erection bobs between the two of us.

"Mhmmm." I moan against her lips as she grips my dick in her hand. Lauren squeezes it just so at the base before she slides her hand up, twisting around my sensitive crown and back down again.

"Fuck," I growl after she does that a few more times, then she drops to her knees and wraps her lips over the head of my cock. My eyes roll back in my head as Lauren takes me further into her mouth. The tingles that run up my spine when the tip of my cock hits the back of her throat and she moans around me almost knock me over.

"Damn, baby." I slide my hands into her hair as I let her keep control, and she sucks my cock until I can't take the pleasure anymore. I pull her up, kissing her hard once she's standing.

I don't let her stay that way long before I'm picking her back up and dropping her on the center of the bed. I fish my wallet out of my pants and remove the condom I made sure was there before I left the house. I quickly rip it open and sheath myself before bringing my hand to her pussy. She's wet and ready for me. I sink two fingers inside her, finding her g-spot and flicking it, making her writhe against my hand. I watch as her pleasure builds, then just before I can tell her body is ready to roll over the edge, I drop my mouth to her mound and suck her clit between my lips. Her body clenches against my fingers hard, and the gasp of pleasure that falls from her lips has me almost coming in the condom before I even sink inside her.

I pull my fingers from her pussy and slide up her body, aligning my cock with her entrance. I thrust in, stopping once I'm balls deep, and feel the ripples of her orgasm still controlling her body. The intrusion of my cock has her moaning out as another shock runs through her. I stay still, allowing her to adjust to me and let her body recover from the intensity of the orgasm.

Once I feel her relax and start to move against me, I find a rhythm and set a steady pace as I make love to her.

"That feel good, sweetheart?" I whisper against her neck as I drop kisses.

"Mhmm," is all the answer I get.

I rotate my hips, hitting her at a different angle, and her moans intensify. I know this angle must be better, as her body's reaction has me speeding up and thrusting harder, bringing us both to the edge and over.

I thrust a few final times, filling the condom with hot ropes of cum. As my body empties, I collapse, doing my best not to crush her under me.

Once I've had a few moments to catch my breath, I pull out, immediately missing the warmth and tightness of her body, and head into the bathroom to clean up and dispose of the condom.

I walk back out to the bed, a warm wet washcloth in my hand.

"Here, I brought this out for you." I hand Lauren the washcloth. "Unless you'd rather take a shower together," I say, kissing her shoulder.

"Not now. I'm too exhausted. Especially now," she says, a

satisfied smile on her face as she tosses the washcloth and settles back on the pillows, pulling the blankets around her.

I pull back the blankets on my side and adjust the pillows before I slide in, wrapping my body around hers. We both quickly drift off to sleep, wrapped up in each other's arms.

30

LAUREN

I wake up, the room still dark, with Sam's warm body next to me. I was so shocked when I walked out of the kitchen at Steven and Renee's house last night to find him standing there in the doorway. I'd obviously missed him since returning from my week with him, but I didn't realize just how much that was until I was back in his arms last night. It's going to suck when he has to return in just a few more days.

I roll out of bed and quietly make my way to the bathroom, shutting the door quietly, and waiting until the lock snicks closed to turn on the lights. I quickly do my business, stopping only to wash my hands and quickly rinse my mouth out with some mouthwash from Sam's bathroom bag, then wipe a warm wet washcloth over my face. I didn't have on much makeup, but it still feels good to get the grime and sweat off my skin from last night.

Once I'm done in the bathroom, I slip back into the bedroom, lifting the covers. I sneak a long look at Sam's naked body. The defined muscles along his torso, those thick strong thighs and biceps that are not huge body-builder type, but large enough you know he works out on a semi-regular schedule. His sinewy muscles do funny things to me and are sexy as hell. I don't mind the view one bit.

Once I finally stop staring at his naked body and slide back into bed, curling up next to him. He's lying on his back, so I place my head on his shoulder and drape one of my legs over his, bringing my hand to rest over the beat of his heart. He stirs slightly, wrapping his arm around me, finally settling his hand against my hip.

I place a chaste kiss against the skin of his chest. "I love you," I whisper into the silent dark room. It's only just before four a.m., so I quickly shut my eyes and drift back to sleep.

I'M AWOKEN A FEW HOURS LATER TO THE FEELING OF WARM wet kisses being dropped along my skin. I squirm at the feeling of Sam's facial hair tickling my sensitive areas as he kisses his way down my body, now paying attention to the underside of my breasts.

"Mhmmm…" I moan as I arch into him.

He kisses his way back up, until he's face to face with me. He takes my lips with his own, giving me one hell of a good morning kiss.

"Morning," he says against my lips.

"Morning," I reply.

"How'd you sleep?"

"Perfect, since I was back in your arms."

"I'd have to agree with that," he says, kissing the tip of my nose.

"What should we do today?"

"Well..." he says, stalling as he shifts me back next to him. "In the excitement of me surprising you last night, I realized I forgot to tell you the news I got yesterday as I was leaving work."

"Did you get the transfer?" I ask, excitement lacing my voice.

Sam nods his head, a huge smile covering his face. "Yep, I'm moving back home in just a couple of weeks. So, I was kinda thinking we could go out looking for a place to rent, if that's something that you still wanted to pursue."

I sit up, looking down at him with a huge smile on my face. "Of course! I'm so excited you'll be back here so soon! Do you know yet if you'll be working out of the small field office here, or in Louisville?"

"I'll be here in Lexington, and might just have to go into the larger office in Louisville occasionally. So, no long daily commutes. I'll be home most nights, here to annoy you," he teases, pulling me close enough to kiss my lips.

"I like the sound of that," I say against his lips.

"Well, with that said, why don't we get moving. Grab some breakfast, drop by your parents' house so you can shower and change, and we can look up some places to go and check out for rent. If we find something, we can even put down a deposit if needed, and get the ball rolling on that. We can even go look at furniture if you want if we find a place we love. I know you don't have any, and some of mine won't be worth paying to move, so we'll need to buy some things."

"Sounds like a plan," I say, rolling out of bed and collecting my clothes.

After we both get dressed and ready to leave, we stop in

the hotel's lobby to grab a cup of coffee and a bagel with cream cheese for me and a breakfast sandwich for Sam. We head out to his rental car and he drives us over to my parents' house.

"Good morning!" Mom calls from the kitchen when she hears the door open. "How was watching Ethan last night?"

"He was perfect!" I say as Sam and I walk into the kitchen.

"Oh, I didn't know you were in town, Sam! No wonder Lauren didn't come home last night," Mom teases us.

"Good to see you, Debra," Sam says, wrapping my mom in a hug. "I flew in late last night and surprised Lauren for a few days. Steven was the only one who knew I was coming in. Her babysitting was his attempt to help me get her to their house, so I could surprise her when I got in late."

"Oh, how sweet. What do you kids have planned for today?"

"We're going to go look at potential places to rent. Sam's transfer was approved, and he'll be back home in just a few weeks!" I tell my mom excitedly.

"That was fast. I bet you guys are excited about the distance no longer being an issue."

"We sure are," Sam tells her, the look of happiness evident on his face as he wraps an arm around my waist, resting his hand on my hip.

"I'm going to go shower and change real quick," I say to the both of them. "Do you want to start looking up some rentals available online or in the paper? I can grab the Classifieds from today's paper for you."

"I'll start with what's online, and if we need more options, we can check the paper."

"Ok, I'll be back down in just a bit," I say, giving him a quick peck on the lips.

"I've got to head out myself," Mom tells us before I leave the room. "You kids have a fun time looking at places, and let's plan on dinner sometime before Sam leaves."

"Sounds good, Mom. I'll text you later if we find anything," I say, turning to head upstairs.

31

SAM

WITH LAUREN UP TAKING A SHOWER AND GETTING READY FOR the day, and Debra gone, I pull out my phone and get to work looking up potential rental properties. I pull up one of the many websites that property managers can list their rentals on, and put in some search criteria that I think we'll want. Two bedroom, one-and-a-half bath, central air, et cetera. I even include the potential of renting a small house, that way we don't have to share a wall with any neighbors if we don't want to, and maybe down the road, we can get a puppy.

By the time she comes back down about thirty minutes later, an overnight bag in one hand, I've got a list of over a half-dozen places I think we should check out. I've successfully already scheduled appointments with about half of them for today, and have submitted requests or left messages with the other places.

"How'd the searching go?" Lauren asks, sitting on the bar stool next to me.

"Good, here's the list I've come up with so far," I tell her.

"These, we have showings at already, and the rest I'm waiting to hear back from to set up something. We never really discussed what we wanted in a place, so was there anything that you specifically wanted in amenities?"

"Laundry either in the unit, or hookups so we can buy our own. I loathe having to take my clothes to a laundry mat or lug them over here to Mom and Dad's."

I chuckle at her. "I hadn't thought of that, but I think most of these places have laundry in each unit. Two of the places are actually small houses."

"Oh wow, I figured a house would be too expensive."

"Most are, but I found a couple that I thought would be worth looking at, to see if we like them. Though, not sharing a wall and having a little more space would be nice."

"When is our first showing?"

"In about a half hour, so we should probably head out and start our search."

A few hours later, we've looked at six places. Three were complete duds. Two were okay, but one was by far the winner of the bunch. It was a two-story townhouse that was built within the last eighteen months. The tenants who moved out were the only people to live in it so far, and the owners had already gone in and fixed the few minor things that needed repaired after they'd moved out. It had everything, plus a few things that were not on our must-have list, like a garage! With an additional pet deposit, they were fine with the potential of us getting a dog down the road. It had a nice little fenced-in backyard, two bedrooms, two-and-a-half baths, and a nice open floor plan on the main level that, even empty, felt homey and perfect.

"I love it," Lauren tells me as we walk through the master bedroom for a second time. It boasts his and her walk-in closets, dual sinks in the master bath, a large walk-in shower, and a soaking tub.

"I do, too. Should we do it?" I ask, pulling her into my side and kissing the top of her head.

"I'm afraid if we wait, it will be gone."

"Then let's do this." I kiss her lips.

We walk back downstairs to where the rental property representative told us she'd wait for us.

"We'd like to fill out whatever paperwork is needed, and put down the deposit or whatever amount is needed to secure the place," I tell her once we enter the kitchen.

"Absolutely!" she says excitedly. "You can fill out the application electronically here on this tablet. It only takes a few minutes for it to process, and then give us an approval or denial. We do have a twenty-five dollar per adult application fee that it will prompt you to pay at the end. Once that checks out, we can sign a lease and get you keys. We do require first and last month's rent, as well as a security deposit. The rent is twelve hundred a month, and the security deposit is the same as the pamphlet states that I gave you when you arrived.

"If you still wanted to think on it, I can also send you with a paper application that you can drop off at the office at your convenience. We go in order of applications received on who gets the unit, if we end up with multiple applications. This listing just became available this morning, and you were the first showing, so if any of the other showings today want to fill out the application, they'll be notified they are in line for it if you guys were to pass on the property, or the showing will be canceled if you sign a lease today."

"Perfect! We don't plan on passing, we love it and think it will be perfect for us," Lauren says as I fill out my portion of the application. I slide the tablet to her to fill out her section before we both sign it in the appropriate places, and I swipe my credit card to pay for the application fee.

"Did either of you have any questions while we wait for this to process?" the agent asks.

"Where do we pay rent each month?"

"We have a few options available. You can set up for an ACH autopay that we deduct from the account you give us permission to, on the first of each month. You can also drop a check off at the office, or have a bill payment check sent directly from your bank. We don't accept cash or money orders. If you want to pay using a debit or credit card, then a three-percent processing fee is added to the rent amount."

"I can run to the bank and get a bank check for the deposit and first and last month's rent as I don't have a checkbook with me," I tell both Lauren and the rental agent.

"I can help cover some of it," Lauren says.

"I know, we can figure that all out later." I drop a kiss to her temple.

The tablet makes a dinging noise, and the agent picks it up with a smile on her face.

"Congratulations, Sam and Lauren. You've been approved! I take it you'd like to head over to the leasing office and sign the lease for this place?"

"Yes, that would be great. We'll run to the nearest bank and be back in just a little bit," I tell her as we all head for the door.

AN HOUR LATER, WE'RE HOLDING THE KEYS TO OUR FIRST place together.

"I can't believe we found a place that quick, *and* already

have the keys to it!" Lauren squeals in my arms as I spin her around our empty living room.

"Believe it, babe, and welcome home. I can't wait to get moved in here with you," I whisper against her ear before I nip at the lobe.

"Mhmmm..." she moans as I kiss along the column of her neck.

"God, I want to fuck you here right now," I growl against her skin.

"What's stopping you?" she sassily asks.

"No condom and no bed."

"Oh," she says, a little deflated. "The 'no bed' thing could make work, the 'no condom' thing, not yet, sorry." She shrugs her shoulders. "I made an appointment with my doctor to go and talk to them about getting an IUD placed. They are safe for women with the clotting issue I have, and would give us a back-up and eventually allow us to ditch the condoms."

"You know it doesn't bother me to have to use one, right?"

"Yes, I just like the idea that we won't have to if we don't want to use one. Allow for spontaneous moments like this to not be ruined."

"Well, what do you say about going out window shopping at the furniture store? I can bring my bedroom furniture, as I bought it all new when I moved into my condo a few years ago. The living room furniture can either come or we can replace it. We'll eventually need to put something in the second bedroom, and get something for the dining room and a couple bar stools for the counter."

"Sounds perfect. But I'm not letting you pay for everything. You have to let me pay for something," Lauren insists.

"Okay, babe. I promise. But I also want to take care of you, and this is one way I can do that."

We head out for the furniture store with a few things in mind for the new place.

32

LAUREN

Sam and I have been at the furniture store for a while already, wandering through all the sections. We found a living room set we both love, so we've decided to just sell off his old set and go with the new one. We also picked out a dining room table and some bar stools. I also found the cutest entryway table that I added to the list of what we're apparently going ahead and buying today.

"We can set up to deliver everything any day starting as early as tomorrow," our salesman, Jake, tells us, as he enters everything into the computer. "Did you have a preference on what day?"

"Tomorrow would be great," Sam tells him, then turns to me. "That way, I'll be here to help you decide where we want things set up."

"That's fine with me," I tell him, as I wait for Jake to finalize the transaction, so we can leave before spending any more money today.

"How was your day?" Renee asks as I help her in the kitchen, getting things ready for dinner tonight. The guys are out on the deck, putting the steaks on the grill.

"Productive, busy, and expensive!" I say on a laugh.

"Oh, how's that?"

"We went looking at rentals, and found the perfect townhome! It's just adorable! I can't wait to have you guys over to see it. It's in that newish rental development off Sixty-Third and Grand. It has a clubhouse with a workout room, and a pool, both indoor and outdoor. They take care of all the yard maintenance and keeping the roads and driveways cleared of ice and snow in the winter. After we signed the lease and got keys, we went and picked out some new furniture we'd need that Sam either doesn't have or isn't worth him bringing with him."

"I'm so excited for y'all," Renee tells me as she rinses the lettuce before placing it in the salad spinner.

"Thanks, it's all happening so fast, but it doesn't feel that way. It just feels right."

"That's when you know it's meant to be. Plus, it isn't like you guys haven't known each other forever. Nice thing about falling in love with your best friend, it just feels right," she says with a knowing look on her face. If Sam and I can make this work between us, like Renee and my brother have made their relationship and marriage work, then I think we'll be just fine. I know they've had their issues here and there, as all couples have, but they've always worked through anything that's come up, and come out stronger from it.

We finish up in the kitchen, each grabbing items to take outside to the deck to join the guys. Ethan is playing away in the bouncer toy that Steven pulled out here for him to sit in and keep him occupied.

"Hey, you," Sam says against my ear, wrapping an arm around my torso and squeezing me in a quick hug.

I smile up at him as I hand him a beer before handing my brother one as well.

"Thanks, Ren," Steven says as he grabs the beer from me. "I hear you guys found a place today."

"Yep, it's great. Once Sam is back, we'll have you guys over for dinner one night."

"Oh, I've already been conned into coming over to help unload the U-Haul truck when this guy arrives with all his stuff in a few weeks. I told him I require beer and pizza as payment, and maybe a babysitting session or two." Steven laughs as he flips the steaks on the grill.

"You know I'll never turn down time with my nephew," I tell him. "Neither will Mom and Dad, you know."

"We know. We're just so tired by the end of each day and week, that going out gets pushed to the bottom of the list of what we actually want to do. We're lucky if we can muster up some takeout and Netflix by Friday night," Renee says.

"Well, the offer always stands," I reply.

We fall into great conversation between the four of us, all taking turns paying attention to Ethan when he demands it from us. We devour the dinner that we all helped cook, and once we've finished, we work together to clean everything up before moving inside to continue our conversation. Renee steps away for a little bit, to get Ethan down to bed, but returns as soon as he's asleep.

We stay for another hour or so before calling it a night and heading back to the hotel.

I check my cell on the way back to see I've missed a few texts from Zoey, so I quickly reply back to her.

Lauren: Hey! Sorry I missed your texts earlier. Sam

surprised me last night and flew in. His transfer was approved, and we went out looking for a place to rent and found the perfect townhome! I'll send you pictures of it tomorrow! We both love it so much!!!

Lauren: We then went out furniture shopping and have a few new pieces being delivered tomorrow! Sam will bring the rest of the furniture when he drives here in a few weeks. I'll be expecting your decorating skills to help me with the rest of the place in the next few weeks!

I drop my phone back in my purse as we pull into the hotel parking lot, and we head straight up to our room. We're both so exhausted from our busy day that we fall into bed, and promptly fall asleep in each other's arms.

33

SAM

3 MONTHS LATER

LAUREN AND I HAVE BEEN LIVING TOGETHER NOW FOR A FEW months. I got everything moved back home and we've settled nicely into our townhome. She's been busy with teaching, and I've been buried in a big case since shortly after arriving and getting settled into the new office. I miss working with Dave all the time, but I've started to make friends with a few of the other agents here. Nothing compares to coming home every night to Lauren, though.

Today is her last school day before we head into the Thanksgiving week holiday. Her district is off school for the entire week, so as soon as she's home tonight, she's off. This will be my first Thanksgiving home in probably five years, so to say my mother is happy is an understatement. My parents are so happy that we finally found our way to each other, which ultimately brought me back home. I stayed away all those years, not wanting to risk running into Lauren and know she couldn't be mine. I thank God every day that changed. She's my perfect other half, and I couldn't imagine doing life without her next to me now that we're together.

Being back home and getting to see my parents on a more regular basis has been great. I know it bothered my mom especially, that I didn't come home to see them very often over the years. Now we've started having dinner with them at least once a week, sometimes more, if our schedules allow for it. Sometimes it's just with them, and other times it's with both sets of our parents, or even Lauren's grandparents, and Steven, Renee, and Ethan, as well.

Sam: Hey, are you leaving right away once school lets out or do you have to stay late?
Lauren: I'll be leaving in about 10 minutes, are you off yet?
Sam: Yep, just got home.
Lauren: Perfect. I need to stop at the store, I want to get it out of the way before the shopping craziness of the weekend happens. Do you want to come with me?
Sam: Sure, swing home and then we can go out to dinner tonight when we're out and about.
Lauren: Sounds good. See you soon. 🌀

Knowing she'll be home soon, I quickly head upstairs and change out of my work clothes, storing my gun in the bedside safe.

We still haven't fully furnished the house since moving in, but Zoey did help Lauren with a few decorating ideas that have helped turn this house into a home. I brought the full U-Haul of furniture from my condo back in North Carolina, which finally sold this week. With all of our family living around us, we don't really have the need for a guest room, so for now, we're just leaving the second room empty. Who knows, maybe we'll be ready to add a baby to the mix in the next couple of years, and that room can become a nursery, if we don't buy a house first. We have all the basic things and rooms furnished. And we love having our friends over on the weekends.

"Honey, I'm home!" Ren calls from downstairs after she walks in from the garage.

I hop off the bed and head downstairs to meet her.

"Hey, babe. Have a good day?" I ask, bending down to kiss her hello.

"Yes, the kids had fun with the Thanksgiving feast and festivities. Everyone was ready for the break next week, so no actual schoolwork got done today, but that's okay, we had fun."

"I'm ready to have a stay-cation with you," I tell her, pulling her body flush with mine. I wrap my arms around her and rest my hands on her lower back. She slides her hands along my sides before snaking them around me and lays her head against my chest.

"Me too," she says on a sigh. "I'm glad you were able to take off next week. How's the case going that you've been working on?"

"Still going. I know they got the one guy to flip and got more information out of him. When I left today, they were putting a plan into place to hopefully arrest two more people involved in the next few days."

"That's good."

"Yep. Are you ready to head to the store now?"

"Let me go change quickly, and then we can head out."

I drop a kiss to Lauren's lips before she can pull away from me to go upstairs. "Love you," I whisper against her lips before she does just that.

"Love you more," she calls over her shoulder as she walks up the stairs.

"I don't think so, babe."

It's a game we play, trying to decide who loves who more.

I'm just thankful we are able to express our love for each other so easily. Hiding it for so many years was depressing, and it being out in the open has made me one hell of a happy man.

Lauren

"I JUST NEED A FEW ITEMS TO MAKE A PUMPKIN CHEESECAKE. Do we need anything else while we're at the store?" I ask Sam as I read through the recipe for the cheesecake and write down the few things we need from the store.

"We have a few things written down on the whiteboard that we need, that you can add to the list," Sam tells me from across the kitchen.

After completing the shopping list, I grab my purse and slide back into my boots, ready to head out.

"Ready?" I ask Sam.

"I was born ready, babe," he teases me, smacking my ass and dropping a kiss to my lips.

"Ugh, you're such a man sometimes." I laugh at him.

"Like you're complaining," he retorts, wiggling his eyebrows at me, causing me to bust out laughing at him.

"I never said that," I tell him as we head out to the garage and climb into his truck.

The grocery store is already packed, everyone trying to beat the rush for the holiday next week. We're slowly making our way up and down the aisles, when we turn down the one with the baking items, and I hear my name being called out.

"Lauren."

I bump into a cart by accident, startled. I'd recognize

that voice anywhere as I look up and see Brad standing just a few feet away.

"Brad," I say, almost on a whisper. I'm a little shocked this is the first time we've run into each other since the last time I picked up things from the condo after I returned from the beach with Sam.

"Sam." Brad reaches his hand out to him. "It's good to see you. I hope things are going well for the two of you?" he asks, and actually looks like he means it.

"Thank you, and the same for you. Are you headed back home for the holidays to see your family?" I ask, finding my manners.

"Yes, we're flying out on Tuesday," he replies, and that's when I notice the woman standing next to him, her fingers laced together with his.

"Oh, hello. I'm Lauren," I say to her in an awkward greeting.

"Lauren, this is my girlfriend, Katie. Katie, this is Lauren and Sam."

"It's nice to meet you. It was nice to see you, and I'm glad you look happy, Brad," I state quietly, as a sort of peace offering. "I really didn't mean to cause you any pain, and I hope you don't hate me for what I did."

"No hard feelings, Ren. It hurt at first, but I think you did the right thing, and I can't ever fault you for that. I wish the two of you all the best," he tells me before we separate and head in opposite directions. I blow out a huge breath I didn't even realize I'd been holding.

"Well, that went better than I expected," Sam says, a few moments later.

"It really did!" I say on a laugh, all the tension draining from my body. I knew the time would come where we'd run into each other, but I never expected it to go that well.

Sam pulls me into a quick hug, dropping a kiss to my temple. "You didn't do anything wrong by following your heart and not marrying him. Always remember that."

"I know. And I wouldn't change my decision for anything, because look where that got us. And I know you're who's held my heart for so many years. I feel complete when I'm with you."

Sam drops his lips to mine, giving me a quick kiss. We are in the grocery store, after all. We continue to fight the Friday night crowds in the store, and finally make our way out to the truck. We stop at one of our favorite sushi places for some dinner before heading home for the night.

34

SAM

9 MONTHS LATER

I can't believe Lauren and I have officially been together for a year now. The time flew by in the blink of an eye. We've had a pretty spectacular year together, falling more in love with each other as each day passes. Moving in together was a small learning curve, but one that we learned together and made us stronger as a couple, and our friendship that much stronger, as well.

Over Lauren's spring break, we took a trip down to North Carolina to see Dave and Meg, and meet their new little baby girl, Rebecca. She was the sweetest little thing and seeing them with a baby was the perfect moment. Knowing the heartbreak, they went through a few years back, and to see the joy on their faces now that they have a baby to raise, was one of the best moments. Lauren and Meg are still great friends and text often to keep in touch. I keep hounding Dave to put in for a transfer to this office, and I might have him convinced with the supervisory position that just opened here that he'd be perfect for.

Tonight, though, Lauren and I will be going out to celebrate our anniversary. I've got big plans tonight, many she's in the dark on.

"Good morning, handsome," Lauren says as she rolls over to kiss my cheek and cuddle up against me. I'd woken up early and just stayed in bed, running this evening's festivities through my head, praying she'll say yes to my proposal. I'm not sure why I'm so nervous, but I am.

"Morning, beautiful. How'd you sleep?"

"Perfect, you had me orgasm drunk," she says on a sigh, and I chuckle at her dramatics.

"I could get you back to that state right now, if you'd like," I tell her, rolling us over so I'm bracing myself over her body, the only body parts touching are my pelvis to hers. My cock is already hard and barely rubbing against her clit.

"Mhmmm..." Lauren moans as I slowly rotate my hips, sliding myself along her mound, feeling her arousal start to coat my cock as I slip up and down her seam.

I shift my hips and slowly push inside her, inch by inch, until I'm fully seated. I don't wait long before I find a rhythm we both enjoy.

Lauren getting an IUD was a game-changer in our sex life. Being able to slide into her bare anytime, that intimacy just did things to me.

"Harder, Sam," she instructs, and I obey. I lift her hips, so I can thrust in deeper, hitting her where she needs it to bring her over that crest, and feel as her body pulls my own release. I collapse on the bed, making sure not to crush her underneath me as I lie here, sated from the hormones rushing through my bloodstream from that orgasm.

"I love you. Happy anniversary," Lauren says on a soft breath.

I reach out, lacing our fingers together. "Right back at ya, babe."

We lie there for a little while longer, neither one of us wanting to move from the warm cocoon of our bed.

"I'm going to take a shower, are you joining me?" she finally asks, sitting up and staring down at me.

"I wouldn't miss that for anything," I tell her, cupping the back of her neck and bringing her down closer to me so I can kiss her.

Lauren

TODAY HAS BEEN PERFECT. SAM AND I HAD A LAZY SEXY morning, followed by a late brunch and a hike afterward. We capped off the afternoon by stopping by a dog rescue to see what they had available for adoption. We'd been discussing getting a dog for months now, but just hadn't found the perfect match for us. We'd gotten into a good habit of stopping in here every week or so, to see what new dogs they had. We thought we'd found the perfect dog a few times, but were just a little too late getting our application in to adopt and they'd gone to other families first.

"Hey, guys!" Debbie, one of the volunteers, greets us as we walk in. "Back to see who's new this week?"

"Absolutely!" I reply.

"I have the perfect pup for you two. She's just become available this morning, so you'd have a good chance at getting her, if she fits your needs," Debbie says as she leads us back to a kennel.

"This is Lucy. She's two years old and was an owner surrender. The guy who owned her had to move into a nursing home and couldn't take her with him. She's up-to-date on all shots, was spayed already, and was well taken care of."

I open the kennel and Lucy comes right out and up to me. She's the sweetest dog I've ever seen, and I know right away that the wait was worth it. She's perfect for us.

"What kind of dog is she?" Sam asks Debbie.

"A true mutt. She's got some German Shepard in her, but also some lab. She's been checked out by our vet and watched under our standard quarantine for five days. She really is a sweetheart of a dog. Well-trained. She definitely misses her prior owner, but appears to take well to new people, as you can see," she says as Lucy cuddles right up into both Sam and me.

"I love her already," I tell Sam. "I think she'd be perfect. Please tell me you feel the same." I plead with my eyes for him to feel the same way.

"I think she's perfect," Sam tells me, a smile on his face. "Debbie, we'd like to fill out the paperwork to adopt Lucy."

"Oh good! I'll go grab it right now. You two just stay here with her."

"I sure hope you come home with us," I say to Lucy as I kiss the top of her head. She's completely calm with us, having laid down next to me, her head in my lap.

"Oh, isn't that the sweetest," Debbie says when she returns and sees the way we're sitting. "Here you go, Sam, you know what to do."

She hands Sam the clipboard with the application on it. He quickly fills out everything and hands it to me to sign. Debbie takes it and comes back just a few moments later.

"I've pushed it through and we've approved you! We already knew you guys were the perfect candidates. Just needed to find you a dog that hadn't already been approved to someone else first. You can take her home as early as today, if you'd like."

"Perfect. We'll need to go get a kennel and supplies, and then we can come back to pick her up," Sam tells Debbie.

We say our goodbyes to Lucy, promising to be back as soon as we can. We pay our fees, and then head for the pet store, buying everything we can think of that we'll need to bring a dog home with us today.

A few hours later, our house is full of dog items, and I'm sitting on the floor with a happy dog in my lap. Sam is behind us on the couch, and we're both in heaven, loving on our new addition.

"Happy anniversary, babe. I think Lucy was the best addition to our family, and the best present we could have asked for today."

"I'm glad we found her," he tells me, reaching down to pet her head.

We stay like that, loving on our new girl for a while, until it's time to get ready for our dinner out tonight with all our family.

Sam

DINNER HAS GONE BY WITH LOTS OF LOVE AND LAUGHTER. Everyone here, except Lauren, knows what's about to go down, and I'm hopeful that we've kept it in the dark. She hasn't let on at all today that she knows or thinks that the proposal is coming, so I'm praying it will be a surprise to her.

Once the servers clear all the dishes from our meals, they bring out the dessert menus and take our orders. While we wait for the dessert to be brought out, my moment has arrived.

I stand and raise my glass, clearing my throat to get everyone's attention.

"I'd like to thank you all for coming out tonight to celebrate Lauren and I. We wouldn't be here if it wasn't for all of you around us. We appreciate all the love and support that you have shown us in the last year," I say to everyone, looking around the room at all our family. I reach for Lauren's hand and pull her up to stand next to me, maneuvering us so we're standing behind our chairs and they'll be out of the way.

I turn to face Lauren, taking both of her hands in mine. She looks up at me with big open eyes, and I think the reality of what's about to happen is hitting her as I see tears start to form in her eyes.

"Lauren. I've loved you since the day I met you, when I was just nine years old. I loved you from the sidelines for many years, standing by your side as one of your best friends. I loved you through the years we were apart, but most of all, I've loved you more and more each of these days from the last year that I've been able to show you and tell you about that love as my partner." I stop only long enough to drop to one knee and grab the box from Steven's hand, who strategically sat next to me and held on to this for me tonight.

"Lauren," I say, opening the box and turning it so she can see the ring, "will you make me the happiest man and marry me?"

The gasp that leaves her lips has my heart skipping what feels like a thousand beats before she cries out, "Yes! *Yes! Yes!*"

I practically rip the ring from the box and slide it onto

her finger, then stand and lift her into my arms. Her legs wrap around my waist as I kiss her hard. I faintly hear the cheers from our family and friends that surround us, but mostly, I just hear her voice over and over saying yes!

"I love you so much," I say against her lips, after we break our kiss.

"I love you, too. I can't believe you just did that."

"Well, I did, future Mrs. Cole."

"I like the sound of that." She giggles before I set her back down on her feet.

We're engulfed by hugs and congratulations from everyone before we settle back down to eat our desserts. I don't let go of Lauren's hand under the table for the rest of the evening. Feeling that ring—my ring—on her finger has me feeling something I've never felt before, and I wouldn't change it for the world.

EPILOGUE

LAUREN

One month later

THE PAST MONTH HAS FLOWN BY IN A WHIRLWIND. BEING engaged to Sam was everything I dreamed of, but marrying him was my end goal. We decided within a day of getting engaged that we didn't want to wait, and with neither one of us really wanting a large wedding, we buckled down and planned it all within a month.

I'd be getting my dream wedding to my best friend. My grandparents' property, my grandfather officiating the wedding, magnolia flowers, just a few friends and family members, and best of all, Sam.

At last night's rehearsal, I never once felt the hesitation I had when I was in this position about to marry Brad. I've moved on from the guilt I held on to for a while from that ordeal, and I'm happier today than I could have ever dreamed of being.

"Ready to go, sweetheart?" my dad asks from the doorway.

"Absolutely. I can't wait!" I pick up my small bouquet and walk toward him.

"I've dreamed of this day for many years. You look more beautiful than I could have ever imagined. Sam is one lucky man," my dad tells me.

"Thank you, Daddy. I feel pretty lucky myself."

We walk out, my arm linked in his, as he escorts me out of my grandparents' house and outside. We walk the short distance of the makeshift aisle, where Sam meets us, and I'm sure the smile that's filling his face matches the one on my own. I love this man with everything I am.

"You look amazing," Sam whispers to me as my dad steps away from us. "I love you."

My grandfather starts the ceremony and before we know it, he's pronounced us husband and wife. Sam's arms surround me as he dips me, bringing his lips hard against mine as he claims me in a scorching kiss. I can faintly hear the hoots and hollers from our family and friends as we finally come up for air. With our hands linked above us in victory, we make our way back down the aisle.

Being that the school year started a few weeks ago, we're waiting to take a honeymoon until a later date. That was our one sacrifice with planning our wedding so quickly, and not waiting to get married until next summer when I'd be off. But we realized it was more important to us to be married than to go on a honeymoon right away, so that's what we did.

***

"Good morning, husband," I whisper against Sam's chest the next morning, and giggle slightly.

"Good morning, wife," he replies.

Lucy chooses that moment to jump up on the bed, letting us know she's also awake, making us both laugh.

"Off the bed," Sam tells her, and she jumps down. "I guess that means we need to get up and feed her. So much for staying in bed for a few hours." He groans.

"We can always come back to bed!" I remind him.

"I like the way you think," he says, dropping a kiss to my lips before he rolls out of bed.

Sam

MARRYING LAUREN YESTERDAY WAS EVERYTHING I COULD HAVE dreamed of and more. When I first saw her walk out of the house on her dad's arm, I forgot how to breathe, knowing she was walking to me.

To become my wife.

It did something to me.

She looked like an angel.

Seeing her glowing in the simple white dress she found a couple weeks ago on a sales rack, with the magnolia flowers, on her grandparents' property. Everything was exactly how she wanted it. I was back in a black suit, sans the flask of whiskey this time, seeing as I wouldn't need it to get through this wedding ceremony.

I was getting the woman.

The one I'd loved for *twenty years* and planned to love for the rest of my life, and longer.

THE END

AFTERWORD

I hope you have enjoyed this book, and you would consider leaving a review on your favorite retailer.

If you would like to connect more with Samantha, please join her reading group on Facebook!

https://www.facebook.com/groups/1233417193443321/

COMING SOON

Protecting Her Heart
Indianapolis Eagles Series Book 4
November 1, 2018
Add it on Goodreads today!
Synopsis coming soon!

ACKNOWLEDGMENTS

There are always so many people to thank when I get to the end of a book.

My husband and kids, for giving me the time away from them to sit in front of my computer screen (or iPad most of the time!) I spent many hours of our family vacation this summer while my husband drove us from place to place with my iPad and keyboard propped up on my lap as I tapped away at the keys to get this story down. Thank you to my three favorite men for encouraging me along the way. For bringing me food and drinks so I could keep in the zone, and for loving me along the way. The encouragement I get from you is what keeps me going! I love you all!

Next comes my team. From my PA and group admins, to my editing, beta, and proofreaders. Thank you all for your feedback, ideas, and help to polish this book to be the best that it can be! I couldn't do any of this without you all! My team is small, but it is mighty!

Thanks to Mignon at Oh So Novel for the amazingly beautiful cover! This was not the original cover that I was intending to use for Marry Me! I already had another cover purchased, but when she posted this one, it just fit perfectly (don't worry, that other cover works perfect for another book coming out next year! 😊)

Give Me Books & the bloggers!!! THANK YOU FOR EVERYTHING YOU DO! You are amazing, and I love each and every one of you! Thank you for pimping out my books, for every post, tag, and time you recommend any of my books means the world to me!

READERS! You are really the rock stars here! And I leave you for last to thank, because as the saying goes: You leave the best for last! THANK YOU SO MUCH FOR EVERYTHING! If it wasn't for you loving my words and buying my books, telling your friends about them, sharing them on your social media etc., I wouldn't be able to do this. So once again, I thank you from the bottom of my heart!

Xoxo

Samantha

ABOUT THE AUTHOR

Samantha Lind is a contemporary romance author. Having spent the first 27 years of her life in Alaska, she now calls Iowa home, where she lives with her husband and two sons. She enjoys spending time with her family, traveling, reading, watching hockey (Go Knights Go!), and listening to country music.

Connect with Samantha in the following places:
www.samanthalind.com
samanthalindauthor@outlook.com

Reader Group
Samantha Lind's Alpha Loving Ladies
Good Reads
https://goo.gl/t3R9Vm
Bookbub
https://goo.gl/4XyyLk
Newsletter
https://www.subscribepage.com/SLNL

facebook.com/SamanthaLindAuthor

twitter.com/samanthalind1

ALSO BY SAMANTHA LIND

Indianapolis Eagles Series:

Just Say Yes - Book 1

Scoring The Player - Book 2

Playing For Keeps - Book 3

Standalone Titles

Tempting Tessa

Until You ~ An Aurora Rose Reynolds Happily Ever Alpha
Crossover Novella

Made in the USA
Lexington, KY
22 September 2018